GEORGE ANDERSON

OTHER WORKS BY PETER DIMOCK

A Short Rhetoric for Leaving the Family

GEORGE ANDERSON

*Notes for a Love Song
in Imperial Time*

Peter Dimock

Dalkey Archive Press
Champaign | London | Dublin

Library of Congress Cataloging-in-Publication Data

Dimock, Peter, 1950-
George Anderson : notes for a love song in Imperial time / Peter
Dimock. -- 1st ed.
p. cm.

ISBN 978-1-56478-801-6 (pbk. : alk. paper)
1. Book editors--Fiction. 2. Synesthesia--Fiction. I. Title.
PS3554.I4394G46 2012
813'.54--dc23

2012033347

Partially funded by a grant from the Illinois Arts Council, a state agency

www.dalkeyarchive.com

Cover design and composition by Mikhail Iliatov
Printed on permanent/durable acid-free paper and bound
in the United States of America

For Wendy

Freedom from torture is an inalienable human right.

—George W. Bush, July 5, 2004

Dear David Kallen,

My name is Theo Fales. In the vision I had two years ago I came to the end of myself and found other people standing there—and knew that the present was a gift of time in which to sing a true history of equal historical selves. That's why I'm writing you now—to request an interview. We were undergraduates together at Harvard though our paths never crossed. I was two years ahead of you.

I need to speak with you. In December of 2004, you signed on behalf of the Office of Legal Counsel the document that contained a footnote that found the policies and acts of torture committed by the officials of the George W. Bush administration legal. Your signature made torture the official policy and accepted practice of my government.

You did this after you directed Special Forces trainers to torture you. Rightly you did this in search of an experiential basis for the words of your legal finding. In the event, you named what they did to you as torture and immediately ordered the procedures stopped with a special hand signal your torturers had given you for that purpose.

Then on December 30, 2004 you signed the official

memorandum you were charged with drafting to replace the secret one of August 2002 that had been withdrawn after it was made public in the wake of the disclosure of the Abu Ghraib photographs. You allowed a note (footnote 8) to be inserted (did you craft it yourself?) that found all previous authorizations of torture to be legal under the standards your words and your experience gave you the art and ability to know.

I need to speak with you in person because I do not know how to live this history. My complicity summons angels singing—I know that you and I are the same person. Somehow our entitlement to rule continues. Surely this is mystery in need of colloquy.

I am requesting the touch of your words in the moving air (and the touch of your hand) in the hope that they will help me learn to live my complicity honorably. I send you this historical method in good faith.

I believe we will soon have the opportunity to meet in person. In four months, on June 19th, both of us are scheduled to attend, as I understand the arrangements, the dedication ceremony and public opening of the new Charles Jason Frears Memorial American Music Archive and Performance Center on the New Carrollton campus of the University of Maryland.

You did something braver than I will ever do. This method I am sending you takes a month (thirty or thirty-one days) to practice in its entirety. We both have the necessary time to prepare ourselves. I use the words my method brings me to create notes for another history. I trust you will agree that history is a discipline of action applied to events in time. You and I know enough to claim the original sovereignty— or, if necessary, a new one—of the authorized grace of a word's reciprocity.

I admire you more than I can say—for your bravery and

for the formal, rigorous beauty of your legal art. You needed an experiential foundation for each word in the crucial legal phrase "the intentional infliction of severe pain or suffering, whether physical or mental" in the Convention Against Torture signed by President Ronald Reagan in 1988 and ratified by the United States in 1994. There had been no rulings about these words in case law. If we become friends, I hope you will tell me if you were convinced that the administration you served needed to extract information from the living bodies of the captured and detained by more active means than previously had ever been permitted by the laws of war?

When we meet in June, both having practiced at least some of the exercises prescribed by this method to the best of our abilities, I propose we discuss the appropriate speech to choose for the history we are now living in the New World.

Was it David Addington, General Counsel for Vice-President Cheney, or another of his aides, who dictated the paragraph of footnote 8 that was inserted after your draft had been reviewed by his office? That footnote stated that nothing in the official legal finding the reader was engaged in reading—your empirical experience of waterboarding with your body to give the word "torture" in the language of the law experiential accuracy and validity notwithstanding—was to be construed to suggest that anything that had been done to detainees at the order of the highest officials in the administration in the seventeen months between August 2002 and December 2004 would not be permissible according to your document's legal reasoning. Torture needed only the sound of your voice before the reader's eyes to be condemned or upheld in law. You signed this memorandum of legal understanding that had the force of law in all offices of the executive branch knowing your signature, once the document included footnote 8, perpetrated war crimes. Why lend the sound of your voice on the page to crimes against humanity given everything you knew and know?

Footnote 8 meant that the methods the Special Forces trainers used on you at Fort Bragg have continued to be used during interrogations conducted under the color of law by American citizens and professionally trained personnel ever since.

By signing that document you undid the truth you knew. I'm not blaming you. I do the same with every breath. There can be no discernable line between public and inward voicing unless actions can be made accountable in speech. Like you I am a loyal citizen and faithful servant of empire.

I cannot distinguish myself from you. That's why I ask now for the chance to meet in person and to speak with you formally but without restraint.

How do we devise a method for living the present moment within a frame of redemptive, universal history? (Our training gave us the rhetorical means to make the case that this was both possible and necessary.) Weren't we taught well that it was our duty to use our power and privilege to dispel all temptations to the contrary? The community of equally valuable free selves was and is the final goal of the American state under our stewardship. The brightness of American summer air—over Bar Harbor or Nantucket—confirms each year the naturalness of our authority.

I know I have no right to ask you to answer these questions sincerely and truthfully unless I am willing to give an accurate and true account of myself.

I have been trying to find a way to do this responsibly during the past few years—to devise a method that won't waste time or encumber others with false, awkward, or wasted mental steps.

During this same time, I am confident I have adequately

met my obligations as Senior Executive Editor for McClaren Books, even serving briefly as Executive Vice-President of the education division for our parent company, NCI Corporation (formerly Newmark Communications International). Now I am sending you my historical method so that my request for an hour to meet in person this coming June 19th will be understood by you as made with a carefully disciplined and rigorously practiced good faith.

Even if you find that you cannot honor my request, my method, if you engage the exercises it prescribes in an active way, will give you a reliable technique with which to weigh the value of my arguments against your own experience. I can say in its favor that there have been moments in my practice of its exercises when I have been able to find myself outside the cycle of owning everything and of fathers killing sons. I rely upon the trust and good faith instilled by our training. I am confident you will take this letter seriously. At my method's end I hope both of us will have a way to approach the people waiting in Fallujah to talk with us about the common history we have made.

≈

Like a name—like empire—this happens all at once: some new speech, some new immediacy of obedience and rule.

By historical method I mean every exercise possible— physical and mental—by which the self can learn to rid itself of inordinate attachments to empire and, once they have been removed, search and find ways to refuse empire and create reciprocity among equals.

This is what happened to me:

This intrusion of a sense of harm in the moment: this

complicity of presence. There are lots of ways of being protected—this system of alarm at the way we rule: all the colors of the world fly loose—they fly calmly toward the screen, then suddenly return to narrative purpose but establish rule by traveling in the wrong direction.

I promise that I'm trying to say what happened as clearly as I can. What happened has determined my system of composition. Without a way of saying it adequate to the occasion there will be nothing but confusion.

This presence of harm:

Mary Joscelyn took a job straight out of Fordham College in the publicity and advertising department of McClaren Books (this was in 1964), a well-regarded mid-sized New York book publisher known for its excellent American history titles. She never worked for any other company and died of a sudden heart attack on a Sunday afternoon in 1995 in her Queens home at the age of sixty-five. She had risen to the position of director of print promotion and was in charge of all print reviews and print media relations for the McClaren imprint. I myself was taken on at McClaren Books as an acquiring editor in 1984 after a ten-year reading binge. (I was a graduate student in American history at Yale.) I was expected, because of my background, to acquire titles in American history and politics. I was permitted to acquire fiction in addition if I could find the time for it. Mary and I did not know each other well. I cannot really say we were friends. How I wish that I could. I like to think we shared a belief in the virtues of elegance and restraint: Jamaican and New England light—so piercing it can sing. That's what I like to think now. This thought needs discipline.

By 1995 McClaren Books had been bought by NCI. McClaren Books and then Lessing & Company Publishing had been added and combined under the McClaren name to become NCI's high-end trade book publishing division world-wide. NCI's human resources department had chartered a bus to take any employee who wanted to go to Mary's memorial service to Saint Sebastian Roman Catholic Church in Queens. Everyone who spoke—daughters, sister, a brother, pastor, Frank Braithwaite, NCI's Vice-President for Media Relations and Mary's boss—spoke of Mary's religious devotion. I had not known of it during all the years we spoke and joked. We enjoyed each other's company and helped each other do the best for the books we worked on together.

Toward the middle of the service—the choir was singing—I felt myself enter through the gates of a vision into my real history. (Tears were streaming down my face; I noticed but did not feel them.) Nothing remotely like this had ever happened to me before. I was raised a secular, upper-class, Protestant child of the American Enlightenment. This precluded all Old World burdens of inherited superstition or the contagion of the unrequited failure of indenture not lived out to term. In my vision I was suddenly four years old again standing behind by mother, clutching in my fists the folds of her black and yellow skirt. The black was the same deep black as a storybook's ink. Across the cloth's billowing undulations marched the most beautiful yellow elephants. In their shining majesty they spiraled around my mother in horizontal lines—strung out according to a joyful informal symmetry of cloth and air—graceful, lifted trunk to delicate, curling tail.

High above—above my arms' ability to reach my mother's waist—appearing in the doorway, was a woman's radiant face—piercing, dancing light shot from behind her head, her hair framed in radiance that flooded the doorway of my parents' New Haven basement apartment.

The woman's eyes were already looking for mine as my

mother's body politely blocked her entrance. How did I know suddenly that the elephants were part of a triumphal procession my mother wore to celebrate her absolute powers of politeness, rage, abandonment, and loss? The woman's eyes found mine there where I stood behind my mother's skirt. They asked without using words—without fear—(they assured me she was willing to bear the knowledge of whatever answer I gave without restraining the reach of my infant terror and glory)—"How are you?"

It was the first empirical question I understood as important. I knew it was urgent beyond sentiment or calculation. In the event (I learned later I had not yet begun to speak though I had just turned four) I answered with my gaze—I could feel the shining elephants marching through my hands—that I was valuable and full of light because she had come back.

In the moment my mother disappeared. (Was this what she had always feared would happen?) I knew she would not let the woman cross the threshold. That would never happen now, nor did the woman expect it. But in the light of Jamaica and New England (or wherever it was my mother had gone and whether or not I would ever be able to find her again) I saw that a New World history of true love was both possible and inevitable. At Mary Joscelyn's service I saw a true vision of another history I had forgotten to live in a way that could be stored and then retrieved from memory.

Then I made a serious error, though I trust not a fatal one. As soon as the service was over, in the joy of my vision's new immediacy, I urgently asked my boss and best friend, Owen Corliss, to give me—then and there—the equivalent scene from his own life. I asked him to tell me what he had seen during the singing. No American lacks this moment: recognizing the person we meet when we come to the end of ourselves and know that everything can be possessed. My vision and now my method have taught me this. Still, I also know now you cannot go around demanding from others the narration of events the way I did. Owen refused—lightly at first. But I insisted. He pretended not to understand; our relations have not been the same since.

My career proceeded—not much changed outwardly, but I knew I could not go on after what I had seen. Then I sleepwalked—I was married and I raised a beloved daughter (well, I hope)—without courage or conviction until 2007.

Then I read about the bravery of what you did to establish the formal, legal meaning, in the Convention Against Torture (signed and ratified by the United States in 1988 and 1994) of the words "severe pain or suffering, whether physical or mental." I knew then (I assume that everyone has the right to assert this right to imaginative, sympathetic knowledge) that, like me, you needed a method for living in the present as a true and universal history to be completed in the New World. Coherence, after all that has been done and said, can have no other source. Together, if we practice a reliable method well, we can find a way to repair what we have done. I have learned to see us standing, an arm's length apart, explaining to people suddenly gathering on a bridge in Fallujah the redemptive logic of American dominion.

By historical method I mean every means by which a person rids the self of its attachment to empire and creates a true reciprocity of equal historical selves. True virtue consists of consent to being in general.

I was able to get your address through Frederick Avery, whose memoir about his time as Director of Central Intelligence I acquired and edited for McClaren Books. As I'm sure you are aware, McClaren and NCI published *Storm Warn-*

ings: War and American Leadership after 9/11 a few years back. (It made it onto a number of bestseller lists for a few, brief weeks.) Fred first told me about what you did and I have read what's been written about it since. Fred is a great admirer of yours. He disagreed, on pragmatic grounds, with the decision to withdraw the previous legal findings under which interrogations of detainees had been conducted, but said, given that decision, you had accomplished with skill, devotion to country, and with enormous courage a very difficult task.

I continue to enjoy the thought and feel amazed at the courage of your action—your decision to find an experiential ground with your own body to establish the legal meaning of the words in U.S. law upholding the enforcement of international sanctions against torture. It is your action that leads me to write to you now. Most people in this country, without acknowledging they are doing so, accept that torture must be used against our enemies because they believe there is no choice but to inflict limitless pain as the price of justified dominance. National security requires torture as a necessary tool to be used responsibly by those entrusted with the stewardship of the limitless, justified power of the American state—civilized empire of last resort.

I know now, because of my vision, that without your action, and others like it, we will not be able to prove to others and ourselves the necessary logic of our virtuous exercise of power. I have written a historical method with which you and I may prove to ourselves and to our loved ones our dedicated pursuit of the public good. Both in principle and fact, that pursuit permits our true love of them. I send you this method in advance of meeting you in person so that together we can devise another history that will repair what we have done.

After reading this, it will be difficult to reach me at my listed McClaren Books address. I have requested and been granted a leave of absence from the company. I needed some time to reconsider my future and to carefully compose this method. This decision comes after continuing difference between Owen Corliss and myself. At one time, I believe, both of us once considered my holding a slightly subordinate corporate title to be merely a formality.

The recent success of Fred Avery's memoir makes me still valuable to the company. Inwardly I now insist on the necessity of acting on a just, historical vision (once its syntax was promised me at Mary Joscelyn's funeral). Owen Corliss has told me this a misplaced personal luxury—one that he says he refuses to indulge at the expense of shareholders. You have done more than anyone else I know to make our present visible as history. With the help of this method and our actions, together I know we will be able to prove Owen wrong. We will be able to do this from within the good faith that clings to the remnants of our entitlement to rule. It's from this that we will make our coherence sing—from this we'll be able to join the logic of our rule to the natural equal rights of others.

Most days I am at my desk in the Reading Room in the Hollander Library at Pace University here in the city. The president and I know each other. We both sit on the board of trustees of the new Jason Frears Memorial American Music Archive and Performance Center whose magnificent new building is just now being completed on the New Carrollton campus of the University of Maryland on the Eastern Shore.

During my leave I have taken it upon myself to use my connections to the several parties to do what I can through research to lay the groundwork for possible mediation to resolve conflicting claims over the performance and licensing rights to some newly discovered Jason Frears recordings of high quality and other materials. These were found in the recent Judith Takes bequest of her personal papers to the Jason Frears Archive. They include the lyrics, once thought to have been lost, to Frears' great four-movement composition, "Light Years." NCI is the parent company that now owns the rights to the recordings Frears made during his most productive and creative years between 1959 and 1964. NCI is the major corporate sponsor of the Frears Center in partnership with the University of Maryland. (We are working on a capital campaign right now to raise an endowment.) Preparations are being completed for the dedication ceremony and public opening to be held in two months time on June 19th. I have been asked if I would make some remarks on behalf of NCI and have agreed to do so. You will be receiving an invitation to this event yourself shortly.

At my desk at the library I have unrestricted access to all the papers and other materials (including rehearsal tapes) from the still uncatalogued boxes given to the Frears Center last year by the terms of Judith Takes's will. My offer to go through these papers and write a report concerning their contents addressed to NCI lawyers and Derek (Judith's son and executor of her estate) has been gratefully accepted. Judith and I were in graduate school together in American history at Yale in the 1970s and 1980s and studied under the same adviser, Professor Charles Quick, a leading historian of early American slavery. I knew Derek slightly as a small boy (I took care of him one summer afternoon when he was six) and saw him occasionally as a young man.

This is how I spend my days now—preparing a preliminary catalog of these valuable new additions to the work of a great American composer. Frears reported that many of his most important compositions, including "Light Years," came to him first in the form of words. He said that once he had found the notes of the music for the words that came to him, the words themselves disappeared from memory. He didn't bother to preserve any record of them; their work was done. Only a few have survived and that appears to have happened by sheer accident.

I have adopted a variation of Frears's compositional technique for this method: The words in which the history of the present we are living first comes to us, we have to assume, are unreliable. The betrayal built into the syntax in which most experience is steeped makes spontaneous speech un-useable for reciprocity. A historical method is necessary to live according to first principles. In the New World we have progressed at least this far: *Every moment forfeit in a history of absolute loss.*

Every moment forfeit in a history of absolute loss: I am valuable because she came back. Memorize this and you will be safe once you learn to create from it a republican, historical method of reciprocity. If I did not have your brave action to rely upon, I would not have any way to assert this or to approach you with any confidence when we meet in Maryland. This will prepare the ground for something to hold onto; some vision to report.

There is a limitlessness to possession of the New World; no settler soul survives intact. No citizen now survives possession's continuance as a lawless entitlement to force.

This is how you began your Legal Finding:

December 30, 2004
Memorandum for James B. Comey, Deputy
Attorney General
Re: Legal Standards Applicable Under 18 U.S.S.
2340 – 2340A

Torture is abhorrent both to American law and values and to international norms.

The following is from an early record of my own practice of this method: Bourgeois good faith finally rests on the ideal of a lasting community of love founded on the ideal of love between spouses. This love—along with autonomy and cultivation—founds a concept of a universal, shared humanity whose freedom of action and reciprocity constitutes the transcendence of modernity without appeal to religion of any sort. Bourgeois freedom establishes the ethical ideal of emancipating an inner realm (operating by its own laws) from extrinsic purposes of any kind. This is the necessary basis for a true history.

If you see Leda before I do, sing her this song so she does not choose another. I am valuable because she came back. I will do the same for you if, while you are away, I meet your one true love and you teach me the words. Refuse empire, create reciprocity inside the present moment with which to build a society of equal historical selves.

≈

The Frears Center board of trustees has invited Leda Corot Rivers to sing at the dedication ceremony and public opening on June 19th. Leda lives in Montreal now and has been invited to apply to be the first Frears Foundation artist in residence for the academic year that begins next fall. I had to recuse myself from voting when the board met. I attended the audition of the finalists held two months ago today and fell in love from the very first notes she sang. I know this is hard to believe, but I assure you it is true. Leda is my one true love. I declare it immediately. Desire must be acted upon. She sang "Light Years" in an arrangement for voice and flute without words.

Leda laughed kindly when I declared myself. She said there was time now that we were no longer young—time in which love could take many forms. I told her I would compose a love song that would prove her wrong. Love, I told her, could only exist in one true action whose independent value was as immediate as the hollow spaces inside a sparrow's wing—all motion a way to cancel loss.

My method takes four weeks and two days to complete. It is divided into four sections, one for each week. The first time through, the first week must be devoted to learning by heart the meditative techniques that will be used throughout; also to memorizing the historical principles underlying the method's effectiveness.

By historical method I mean every means by which a person rids the self of its inordinate attachment to empire and creates reciprocity. The goal is a reciprocity based on an ideal of married love serving as the basis for a just society of equal historical selves. The original logic of the abundance of capitalism was another way of being.

FIRST WEEK

You ordered special forces trainers to torture you so you could establish the legal meaning of the words "severe pain or suffering whether physical or mental." You did this in order to place yourself in a position to revoke beyond appeal your office's previous legal opinion granting permission to the President, Vice-President, and Secretary of Defense of the United States to order torture without fear or threat of prosecution for committing war crimes and crimes against humanity. Your act was brave beyond anything I have ever done. It made and makes another history possible.

But the document you wrote and signed granted immunity to torturers. The document you wrote and signed permitted and continues to permit torture as official policy of the United States against all customary norms and statutes of both domestic and international law. The bravery of your act makes another history possible. (By history I mean some true narrative recounting events of pleasure, force, and love.)

Empire and democracy are not compatible. By what narrative logic do we reconcile them? Whom did you see standing there at the end of yourself as they tortured you? What did you say in your mind to your one true love? How will you declare your love when you read this and when we meet?

First Day's Exercise: Choose some master narrative by which to live other than our present complacent fairy tale of destined consumer's empire. Remember: Whenever any Form of Government becomes destructive of the unalienable natural rights that all people hold equally, it is the right of free persons to alter or abolish it and to institute new Government, laying its Foundation on such Principles, and organizing its Powers in such Form, as to them will seem most likely to effect their Safety and Happiness.

For my master narrative, I have chosen every moment and motion in the life of George Anderson, as these were represented in an article appearing in the Trenton, New Jersey State Gazette on April 6, 1925. (The article is reprinted for your convenience in its entirety at the back of this method. Beside it you will find the complete text you wrote and signed, including footnote 8, of your Office of Legal Counsel "Memorandum for James B. Comey, Deputy Attorney General" dated December 30, 2004 above the heading: *Re: Legal Standards Applicable Under 18 U.S.C. §§ 2340-2340A*.)

The master narrative I have made from these two documents using this careful historical method will serve both of us much better than any other I have seen to date. (I have not ceased looking at the ones others write just because I have written my own. I will, of course, be glad to consider any alternative meditative discipline combining these two documents that you propose.)

Essential to any historical method is a master narrative of presence in which the practitioner learns to sing an accurate love song to his or her one true love. Memorization of the notes of the melody is therefore essential to the task of mutual accountability. There is no other way to lodge an equally valued body inside the abstraction of nationality. Through careful practice of my method's course of exercises, "George

Anderson" is a master narrative now firmly lodged in my memory, and it is continually renewed and can be relived as needed through my method's daily practice.

Here is how my master narrative now begins:

> Up at 501 Calhoun Street there is a little, weather-beaten frame house that sets back from the sidewalk, huddled between two large properties as though trying to hide its shabbiness from the gaze of the passerby. The busy public has no time to take a second look at it, so few know its secret. It is the home of one of Trenton's very richest men.
>
> His wealth does not consist of anything so commonplace as money. If he wanted a dollar right this minute it is extremely doubtful if he could find it anywhere in those worn old clothes of his, but he has a store house, and in it are treasures that only a man who has lived a whole century may possess—it is the storehouse of memory.
>
> While he pursued the humble calling of a farmer time went marching by, leaving in its wake the history of three wars and the advent of the greatest triumphs of a scientific age. Best of all, from his point of view, time brought the abolishment of slavery, treasure of treasures for the storehouse. Now that age has robbed him of his once healthy body he can fall back upon this wealth and distribute it to those about him, and, after all, no man is quite so rich as the man who shares.

Give your master narrative a textual foundation. Commit as many key portions of it as you can to memory so that it has a chance to feed your imagination continuously. Otherwise we abandon each other without restraint. My master narrative is filled with New England and Jamaican light. Our best American philosopher once proved beyond all contradiction that the nature of true virtue is consent to being in general.

The master narratives you and I choose need not agree. The only requirement is that they both distinguish freedom from the impunity of the American imperial state. Both must concede that an empire of liberty has not yet arrived—not in Fallujah, not in Kabul, not in White Plains.

As important as the master narrative you choose is the governing scene you give it. The governing scene is the picture you give your narrative in your mind so that you can hold your narrative in consciousness clearly over a sustained duration or summon it immediately for internal review as the occasion requires.

The governing scene I use is a composite made from two moments taken from the Trenton newspaper article:

George Anderson at the age of twelve is standing and watching—everyone on the Danville farm was ordered by the master to appear in the Fair House yard to witness a slave's correction—from early morning until late in the afternoon, as his brother, older by four years, Robert Anderson, is whipped to death by two men, his master and the overseer. (They whip him continuously, taking turns, for having stolen something after previous punishments and warnings for the same offense had not reformed his character. It is well known by everyone present that Robert is the master's son.) There is an April light in Virginia in which birds' wings flash—Edenic it is called, and then American.

I have captioned this moment with words from the Trenton newspaper article: "So they began to beat him early in the morning."

This first scene immediately gives way and merges with the next one: To the accompaniment of the explosive sounds of the flapping walls of a revival's canvas tent, George Anderson is suddenly standing twelve years after the end of the Civil War explaining to everyone around him that he has found his savior. He is animated and joyful and speaks with great confidence. I have labeled this moment and its duration with the words of the newspaper article, "When I knew I had found my Savior I got right up in that meeting and told everybody so." (The passage in its entirety reads, "When I knew I had found my Savior I got right up in that meeting and told everybody so and since that time I have never been alone. I did not cast off the chains of slavery at the time of the surrender, they fell off at that camp meeting.")

Without control the governing scene can produce the following undisciplined sound instead of a musical note: "No other sound beneath his screaming—this sparrow in morning flight—this white post's new wood—a complicity of presence."

You proved torture with your body and then signed documents granting immunity and insuring that torture would continue as a virtuous policy of the American state. Writing this, I feel my acquiescence and lend my complicity to your signature.

It never occurred to me to insist that Fred Avery deal in his memoir more conscientiously with the question of his responsibility for authorizing and overseeing the torture with which the agency he directed was tasked by those who appointed you to head the Office of Legal Counsel, the post you always dreamed of holding. Of course, he attended all the meetings of principals in which torture's necessity was discussed. His high rhetoric (and boyish laughter)—the devotion of his public service—the stern kindness of his unpretentious command—my complicity—the fellowship of our birth and class—all this prevented it. The stillness surrounding the careful silence of authority is not kind. In the event we decided it was best that the text of his memoir emphasize the intensity of the good faith with which he protected the nation in a time of war. We agreed to stress, with the sound of modest words, his devotion to family and country in the exercise of his disciplined will and fallible moral strength.

I did not question his rhetoric or his narrative. What did you think when you read the passage in his memoirs about lawyers (in a crisis "despite what Hollywood might have you believe, you don't call in the tough guys; you call in the lawyers")? Are all the rest (the acts themselves as knowable experience) authorless events from a dead star committed by no one who need be held accountable so long as patriotic motives governed the speech that gave the order? Did it make present the perfection of the violence and the silence we bear so lightly and so drunkenly inside ourselves? Avery's book sold more copies than any other title in bookstores its first week; it continues to sell well, I'm sure. I am your accomplice in our class's alchemy of national impunity.

Our force of rule, in every moment, extends beyond all law. This is the secret of all totalitarian government.

I'm not blaming you. I have sworn to do the same as you or worse. Neither of us has ever resigned from anything for reasons of principle.

By historical method I mean every means of examination of conscience, of meditation, of contemplation of vocal and mental speech and other acts by which a person prepares and disposes the self to rid its coherence and integrity of all inordinate attachments to empire, and, after their removal, by which he or she creates reciprocity and joins with others in a society of equal historical selves (SOEHS).

To begin is always hardest. The ending, I hope, will come easily and in good time once we have begun. Things happen only once and in only one way. If this were not the case we would not be listening like this to the just reproach of all the anonymous, historical dead.

My father and his father before him fought, painfully, almost famously, in foreign wars. They both killed many men—women and children too. I never came close to doing anything as brave as you. My father was a gentleman and a scholar who said everyone, in principle, owed the state a life. Is this true? In the event, I told him he lied—that he held that doctrine out of self-interest and not to further emancipative, democratic reason. Was I right to make this claim—this buttressed argument? What appropriate action flows from such aggression?

The choice of a new master narrative and a governing scene with which to refuse empire will come easily only for a few. For most it will come with difficulty.

The First Day's Exercise is to write on a loose sheet of paper (or on the line provided below, if you prefer) the master narrative you have chosen with which to live the present moment as history. Next, immediately below this, describe in as few words as possible the governing scene with which you will hold your master narrative in mind over a sustained period. The governing scene should be designed so that it can bring your master narrative immediately to consciousness whenever the occasion demands its use.

Master Narrative:

_____

Governing Scene:

_____

Second Day's Exercise: Now that you have chosen your master narrative and its governing scene, identify the sources you will use in making reasoned arguments to justify your actions in the present. This is the art for which we were trained. (Of course you are welcome, instead of creating a master narrative and governing scene of your own, to adopt mine and adapt them as you wish. Again, the documents upon which the present I am living depend (the longer one was written by you) are both included here at the end. How can we rely upon our words to mean themselves when we meet in person unless we know how our rule is explained as just? The bravery of your action to decide the meaning of words, my vision two years ago, and my daily practice of this method give me hope that we can create the present of another history.

The present, a waiting for justice, takes the form of a love song. It sounds like this:

> *Every moment forfeit/In a history of absolute loss./I am valuable because she came back./If you see Leda before I do,/Sing her this song/So she does not choose another./I will do the same for you, if,/While you are away, I meet/ Your one true love/And you teach me the words./Refuse empire; create reciprocity.*

Third Day's Exercise: If you do not already have them by heart, memorize now the words of the Declaration of Independence. This will assure that the master narrative of our empire will be brought closer to you, giving you a secure place to begin. If you feel the powers of memory waning, memorize as far as the lines "and organizing its Powers in such Form, as to them shall seem most likely to effect their Safety and Happiness. Prudence, indeed, will dictate that Governments long established should not be changed for light and transient Causes." This much will give you a safe and accurate way to proceed. Here are the words again:

> When, in the Course of human Events, it becomes necessary for one People to dissolve the Political Bands which have connected them with another, and to assume among the Powers of the Earth, the separate and equal Station to which the Laws of Nature and of Nature's God entitle them, a decent Respect to the Opinions of Mankind requires that they should declare the causes which impel them to the Separation.

> We hold these truths to be self-evident, that all Men are created equal, that they are endowed by their Creator with certain unalienable Rights, that among these are Life, Liberty and the Pursuit of Happiness—That to secure these Rights, Governments are instituted among Men, deriving their just Powers from the Consent of the Governed, that whenever any Form of Government becomes destructive to these Ends, it is the Right of the People to alter or to abolish it, and to institute new Government, laying its Founda-

tion on such Principles and organizing its Powers in such Form, as to them shall seem most likely to effect their Safety and Happiness. Prudence, indeed, will dictate that Governments long established should not be changed for light and transient Causes;"

Exercises for Days Four through Seven: The rest of this first week will be quite difficult. Do not underestimate the demands its tasks impose upon your concentration, stamina, and intellectual discipline. Devote days four through seven to mastering the rules (by memorizing you will also begin to practice them) by which you both choose and commit yourself to live the present as history.

You will be asked, at first, only to align in contemplation your governing scene with the week's assigned historical subject. The goal is for both the scene and subject to be revealed through the day's exercises in their emancipative dimensions. This goal will be framed and eventually brought to completion by inserting yourself into the master narrative you have chosen.

The most difficult task during these days is the following: The rules of this method prescribe precise procedures for converting contemplative juxtapositions (these are designed to strengthen the powers of memory) into the internal mental sound of a single musical note being sung by a human voice. Each note's timbre, pitch, and duration are fashioned from the application of this method's logic to your meditations using prescribed elements from the method's three tables. (This instruction will become second nature to you after a few days' practice.) You will become intimately acquainted with these tables (and make them your own) during the next four days. This will appear difficult, at first, but I assure you that creating a note's sound in your mind creates the basis for reciprocity upon which another history can proceed.

A historical method of true virtue is necessary to create love songs out of music that comes to you first in words whose syntax has already betrayed you. It will permit you to sing, in the midst of empire, a universal history that includes your one true love.

Through contemplation, memorization, and meditation, begin to practice this historical method by learning its exercises and absorbing its principles as explained below.

Rules for a Historical Method

Master Narrative :_____

Governing Scene :_____

My master narrative is the history of George Anderson, former slave, born on a plantation near Danville, Virginia in 1817 and interviewed by Marion C. MacRobert for an article in the Trenton, New Jersey State Gazette, published on April 6, 1925. The entire article is included at the end of this method.

Table One: Historical Subjects

List here the four subjects you have chosen for the four weeks of this historical method's meditative cycle.

I._____

II._____

III._____

IV._____

Note: During the first cycle of your practice, the first week must be devoted to learning the rules of the method. You will not therefore be able, during your first cycle, to undertake a full meditative engagement with your fourth subject. I have found it best, when beginning the method's complete cycle for the second time, to begin with the first subject and work through the historical subjects in the same order in which they were listed originally. All of us list last the subject in which we place the most hope. For that reason, the fourth subject is the one to which it is important that we bring the most practiced discipline each time we arrive at it.

I have recorded the results of my own practice of this method's exercises during one cycle to provide you with examples against which you can juxtapose your own. This will allow you, when we meet, to have a reliable way to answer or refuse my good faith. I have not been able to say this to anyone before now (I hope to say it to you in person when we meet): The coerced complicity of presence enforced in every moment by our class's rule is unbearable. Patriotic constructions of nationality cannot substitute for justice or justify postponement of history's enlightened dream of natural, universal equality: Freedom is not free when it is used for domination.

Table One: Theo Fales's Historical Subjects
I.   George Anderson, 1817 – 1926 (?)
II.   Derek Takes, 1964 –
III. Judith Takes, 1939 – 1999
IV. Theo Fales, 1949 –

Table Two: Truth Statements

When in my vision I came to the end of myself and found other people standing there, it never occurred to me that others would not believe my account of what I saw. I was unprepared. The truth of vision always appears self-evident. In my relief and joy I made the mistake of demanding from my close friend and colleague there in the church in front of witnesses his account of the equivalent scene from his personal history. The truth I saw in my vision (I was convinced of it then and am convinced of it now) was that every American has his or her own true version of the moment I heard and saw. Another history will be made possible if we say it aloud: Limitless possession in the New World and universal freedom cannot be reconciled.

Speech as persuasion must be used for good. Speech must be grounded in truths the speaker has tested in the body offered in the service of reciprocity. Memorization helps. Memorization assures familiarity with the words when someone speaks of matters held in common by everyone.

In the event history—like empire, like music—happens all at once. This is presence. Meditations on how to act in history occur within historical structures of emergency. The national security state suspends democracy.

The words of our love songs will not mean anything until we find the music with which to make them true. The words with which we collude with empire are used for advantage, not reciprocity.

I have found it useful to memorize seven truths. The application of these truths to the scenes in my mind produces knowledge I hold onto. I hold them in the present with the mental sound of a musical note. This note sounds according to the juxtaposition (early in the morning) of three things: a true master narrative, a historical subject, and a governing scene. Their juxtaposition is arranged and applied in the presence permitted by each day. Presence is made from the promptings of a pair (one in a prescribed sequence of four) of constructive principles. Each pair contains one positive principle, one negative. The eight principles, arranged in their prescribed order and pairings, are given below.

But before I list these pairs, I will provide you a table of the seven truths I myself use in the practice of this method. These seven statements have stood the test of time. I insist these truths have never been contradicted either by reason or experience. A dogmatics of justice in the midst of empire is necessary when a love song is found still to be missing its words.

Table Three: Seven Truths

I.   Every ruling minority needs to numb, and, if possible, to kill the time-sense of those whom it exploits by proposing a continuous present. This is the authoritarian secret of all methods of imprisonment.

II. The most important element of poetics is the structure of events, for tragedy is the mimesis not of persons but of life and action. Happiness and unhappiness consist in action and the goal is a certain kind of action and not a qualitative state. It is by virtue of character that persons have certain qualities, but it is through their actions that they are happy or the reverse.

III.   I would like to arrive at the point where I am able to grasp the essence of a certain place and time, compose the work, and play it on the spot naturally.

IV.   Some discouragement, some faintness of heart at the new real future that replaces the imaginary, is not unusual, and we do not expect people to be deeply moved by what is not unusual. That element of tragedy which lies in the very fact of frequency, has not yet wrought itself into the coarse emotion of mankind; and perhaps our frames could hardly bear very much of it. If we had a keen vision and feeling of all ordinary human life, it would be like hearing the grass grow and the squirrel's heart beat and we should die of that roar which lies on the other side of silence. As it is, the quickest of us walk about well wadded with stupidity.

V.   Whenever events lose their independent value, an abstruse exegesis is born.

VI.   When the whole world is a computer and all cultures are recorded on a single tribal drum, the fixed point of view of print culture will be irrelevant and impossible no matter how valuable.

VII.   At first I was afraid. This familiar music demanded action of the kind of which I was incapable, and yet, had I lingered there beneath the surface I might have attempted to act. Nevertheless, I know now that few really listen to this music.

List on the lines provided the truth statements you will be using in your own practice of this method.

Table Two: Truth Statements

I._____

II._____

III._____

IV._____

V._____

VI._____

VII._____

Table Three: Eight Constructive Principles of Composition
(Arranged in Pairs)

Now I come to the most difficult part of this method. I confess that I myself have misgivings about how easily the rules I specify for the composition of musical notes can be used by others. Nevertheless I have decided to offer these to you until you have chosen others of your own and explained the principles guiding you. As my mother used to say, "You may as well be hung for a sheep as a lamb."

After you decide on generative rules of your own for the sound of your contemplations' notes, I will practice them (if you ask me to) as diligently as I practice my own. Though we may fail to master each other's constructive principles completely, before we meet, the effort to do so will help assure our mutual good faith.

Direction is given after each exercise to create the mental sound and abstract duration of a musical note with which to hold the results of the contemplation clearly and securely in mind. Here is my generative principle: The resonance of a recounted event depends on the directness of expression by which it can be recognized and shared as true.

If this principle is true, history can be imagined within a syntax that has already betrayed its user. The goal is a true love song within New World narratives (mine is of fathers killing sons). There is a new limitlessness to the logic of possession in New World modernity along with the realist doctrine that things happen only once and in only one way.

No historical writ of justice extended beyond the marchlands that a free-holder or soldier in a joint-stock company's pay needed to obey. Absolute possession creates new loves, new men. Jesuits out-Protestanted the Protestants and made plausible from inside events a rational sovereignty of absolute force. (My method is borrowed from theirs.) I claim both logics have been updated by the national security policy doctrine, C4 + I (Command, Control, Communications, Computers plus Intelligence).

CONSTRUCTIVE PAIRS
First Constructive Pair

i(a) [Positive]: The emancipative dimensions of bourgeois literacy and the politics of the Third Estate produced the individual by whom all determining secular value is to be measured and applied. Nationalism sacralizes individual liberty and instrumentalizes it on behalf of empire. Liberal New World history promised and still promises escape through reason from the constraints of what is without appeal to transcendence of any kind. Your written action and my cowardice undo the reciprocity promised by the lettered freedom of event and public narrative our Revolution began to make possible. History is not good-faith narrative of a failure to realize the public good. It is now the unacknowledged order of limitless force administered by an imperial logic of impunity and local Apocalypse.

i(b) [Negative]: Historylessness is now the condition of everyday life. Empire promises in every moment the ecstasy of absolute possession as compensation for a past and future of absolute loss.

Second Constructive Pair

ii(a) [Positive]: It is both necessary and possible to live the one true history of your one true love. Romance's discipline must be exercised with the energies of religion.

ii(b) [Negative]: Under conditions of imperialism, everyone is forced to improvise reciprocity; every moment forfeit until justice can make its claims felt.

Third Constructive Pair

iii(a)[Positive]: The only serious philosophical question is the question of what Eurydice saw when Orpheus looked back. What she sees determines the worth of his song. Mortality trumps aesthetics; lyric follows epic chronologically as form. The king of the dead knew, even as he was letting her go, that he was making a big mistake by being seduced by Orpheus's song. Eurydice is asking what the future holds beyond absolute possession.

The story of honey's origins—the taste of words' sweetness in the mouth—goes like this: A farmer has lost his bees (they have swarmed), and he goes to his mother to ask what has gone wrong. By following his mother's instructions, the farmer learns that Orpheus is punishing him for raping and then killing on her wedding day the girl Orpheus was about to marry—Eurydice. The farmer is told what he has to do to appease the husband who once sang so beautifully.

The remedy: Build a sturdy house, at least eight meters square, made of saplings and mud on a patch of waste, abandoned ground. Each side has to have a windowed opening. Inside beat a steer to death with a wooden club (no blood must show), a rope of hemp around its neck, and leave the carcass until the spring. Enter when the sun is warm, and there, hanging inside the curving cavity of white bone (loose strips of flesh will still be dangling down), you will find a hive overflowing with sweetest honey. Eurydice is forever gone.

iii(b) [Negative]: Temporalities of managed, stochastic determination have ruled events since 1945. Stochastics is that branch of mathematics that concerns random sets of observations each of which is plotted as a point on a separate distribution curve. This technique assures that knowledge has no way to distinguish truth from power: algorithms manage preference backed by force, mathematics suspends choice and replaces politics.

Fourth Constructive Pair

iv(a) [Positive]: The proper goal of an emancipative historical method is a society of equal historical selves (SOEHS).

iv(b) [Negative]: Attend the continuous sound of the roar of reproach from all the anonymous New World dead. (I heard it as a child, holding my mother's yellow elephant-chained skirt.) Allow this sound to accompany your love song inside the hollows of a sparrow's wing in flight.

Note for Table Three: It may prove helpful while practicing this method to use shorthand designations for the Paired Constructive Principles of Composition. Here are the words I have used to name the constructive principles I have chosen and to hold them carefully in mind:

i(a). Emancipative dimensions of bourgeois literacy; i(b). Historylessness;

ii(a). The one true history of your one true love; ii(b). Improvised reciprocity;

iii(a). What Eurydice saw when Orpheus looked back; iii(b). Stochastic temporality;

iv(a). Society of Equal Historical Selves (SOEHS); iv(b). The reproach of all the anonymous New World dead.

When you have chosen your own constructive principles to use instead of mine in your practice of a method, list them in the spaces provided below.

Eight Constructive Principles Arranged in Pairs
(Positive and Negative)

i(a)._____

i(b)._____

ii(a)._____

ii(b)._____

iii(a)._____

iii(b)._____

iv(a)._____

iv(b)._____

SECOND WEEK

First Historical Subject (and Master Narrative):
George Anderson

Dear David Kallen,

Let me now begin again. I hope you will not reject my request for a time and place to meet and speak with you in person. We share the same history. Our personal histories entitle us to positions of comfort and rule. I am an expert by formal training in our national narrative. Over my long career as editor I helped regulate a bourgeois ethical monopoly over the words by which we know ourselves and understand others as universal democratic citizens sharing a modern and Humanist historical good faith.

Who were you when you gave the signal that stopped the trainers at Fort Bragg from torturing you any further? Your action was brave beyond those of anyone else in your or any similar position within the Executive Branch of the American government.

You called torture by its name with the knowledge and authority your body gave you. You wrote a draft of an official finding, writing as acting head of the Office of Legal Counsel whose words had the force of law. You ruled torture to be illegal under U.S. law and treaty obligations no matter what was claimed by historical actors of the executive branch to be the requirements of empire. You then added a footnote—was it forced on you? If so how was that order enforced?—that undid your memorandum's asserted intention to withdraw legal protection from the torture that had been inflicted for years on persons within the control of the U.S. government and, in secret, had been made official policy in August 2002.

Whenever any Form of Government becomes destructive of these Ends (Life, Liberty, and the Pursuit of Happiness). The purpose of this method is to allow us to speak freely when we meet. I write these words and send them to you now to demonstrate my good faith and the sincerity of my request.

The master narrative I have chosen for my own practice is the true history lived out in the biography of George Anderson. Reading is generative—it is a meditative act. Take the time to read again and begin to memorize the Trenton State Gazette article from April 6, 1925 that I have enclosed at the end next to the text of your official legal finding. The article begins, "Up at 501 Calhoun Street there is a little weatherbeaten frame house that sets back from the sidewalk."

Republican government is founded upon the principle of the immediacy of communicative reciprocity.

I very much look forward to our meeting in which we will have the chance to talk. When that time comes, I may ask you for your law firm's legal services on my own behalf, and also, perhaps, on behalf of NCI. I have removed from the papers Judith Takes left in her will to the Frears Center the original of the page, written in Judith's hand, containing previously unknown lyrics to Jason Frears's composition "Light Years." Frears once reported in an interview that "Light Years" came to him first in the form of words. He had written the words down, but they had subsequently gotten lost, and he could no longer remember them.

This often happened, he said. He considered the originating words irrelevant once he had found the music for them on his instrument and had taught the notes and the intervals to the musicians he played with. The music would take care of itself.

I have temporarily removed this document because of the potential for litigation I see arising over legal ownership of the document and the licensing rights to the lyrics themselves. Both Frears and Judith's estates have valid claims, I believe. Since you left the Office of Legal Counsel (Why were you not confirmed as head? Were you not sufficiently compliant?), I know you have made intellectual property your specialty.

The continuous present we impose insults the dead to no good end. It's all forgivable—it's just that the forgiving must be done with the immediacy of a note sung inside the hollow bone of a sparrow's wing in flight. I'm valuable because she came back. This original New World light—in Virginia, Jamaica, or New England—comes neither too quickly nor too late. I look forward to June 19th. Words for your actions could restore the happiness of all the anonymous dead and resolve it into presence.

I know that NCI, by the terms of its commitment to provide sustaining financial support for the Frears Center (NCI is an active corporate participant in Maryland's Public-Private Partnership Arts Initiative Program), holds the licensing and recording rights to all Frears unpublished musical materials owned by the Center's archives. It was always assumed there would be very little of this, given the care Frears took to secure the copyright in his own name to all his compositions in all the recording and publishing contracts he signed. I simply do not want this clause in the corporate giving agreement to unfairly deprive Derek Takes, Judith's son, of income due him as the beneficiary of his mother's estate, if it turns out that "Light Years" was originally composed as a song with lyrics that should be legally credited to both Jason Frears and Judith Takes. In your firm's published biographical profiles of partners, you are credited with recent court victories featuring large awards to plaintiffs in intellectual property trials.

I am hopeful that with your firm's help a negotiated settlement over the licensing rights to the newly-discovered lyrics to "Light Years" can be quietly reached satisfactory to all the parties. I will be happy to do what I can to bring the board of trustees of the Frears Center on board regarding any changes that need to be made in the corporate sponsorship agreement between NCI, the Center, and the University of Maryland as a result of the settlement. Meanwhile I will keep the original document safely in my possession.

I have not yet shared the lyrics with anyone, including Leda, though she intends to perform "Light Years" at the dedication ceremony as a song without words in her own arrangement for flute and voice.

After these preliminaries, it is now time to begin this historical method's daily practice in a systematic way.

During the second week the task of the contemplative exercises is to master the form of your master narrative and make it your own by applying it to daily life. Others have succeeded at this in the past; this used to be common practice. Readers took direction from Thomas à Kempis or Ignatius Loyola or Jonathan Edwards and applied these authors' historical methods to the motions of their hearts. They had the advantage, of course, of time shaped to the rhythm of a biographical template for an exemplary life. We lack that resource. In the New World we committed ourselves to redemption through the freedom of material possession. We asserted the ecstasy of possession without appeal to transcendence of any sort.

I will illustrate this truth from my own experience. George Anderson was one of the persons I found standing at the end of myself when I came to the conclusion of my vision during Mary Joscelyn's funeral in the spring of 1995.

I first read the article about him in a history graduate seminar at Yale with Professor Charles Quick in 1978. I was assisting Quick in compiling for a university press a volume of first-hand testimony by former slaves concerning the experience of slavery in North America. The tentative title of my dissertation (never completed) was "Historical Narrative and the Subjectivity of New World Slavery."

Professor Quick's response to my proposal was sympathetic but skeptical. Once, when I was talking to him about my argument, he laughed freely and called my position "Neo-abolitionist." I felt suddenly unmasked—but why did I also feel disabled?

It's true I'm a Northerner—a New Englander after all—despite all the years I have spent in New York City.

I had already been listening to Frears's music in a desultory way when I came across the 1925 Trenton State Gazette article. I was then far from being able to commit myself to lyric as a principle of historical composition. I know now that it's our investments in slavery—I mean investment in each and every one of its forms—that makes us confuse freedom with empire. Investments in slavery and its legacies prevent any accurate narrative of democratic New World enlightenment from which to create reciprocity.

First Day's Exercise (Historical Subject: George Anderson): The first day's exercise is to confirm through meditation within an un-coerced discipline of thought your reasoned choice of a master narrative. The method's rules insist that you stick with your choice for the entire month's cycle, however difficult your thoughts may become during any day's exercise.

The purpose of this rule is to give you direct experience in refusing the master narrative offered by empire's ordinary day. Success comes with your ability to develop a governing scene, no matter what is happening, with which to bring your master narrative urgently to mind whenever it is needed. This holds true whether you are in the midst of contemplative exercise or going about your ordinary business.

By way of illustration I offer below my own governing scene constructed from the published version of my master narrative that you have already read. (I am not trying to impose my own imaginative procedures on you. I am looking to construct a common place of understanding—to make possible a mutual duration—a place holding made from words. This will save us both considerable time when we speak in person.)

The governing scene I use to summon my master narrative to consciousness is a composite image derived from two moments in the Trenton, New Jersey State Gazette article published on April 6, 1925.

Here is the first moment:

> My master was a minister. He was a strict man who preached every Saturday and Sunday and on the other days gave his attention to the farm. If he thought a black man needed flogging he'd tie him to a post and do it himself if the overseer was busy. One day my brother stole something. It was not the first time; he had been

punished for it before, and the master said that this time he should have a lesson he would never forget. So they began to beat him early in the morning. . .."

Some splintering of new light in which the day came to him—a new post in the yard—the post's soft wood—something to witness but not to know. Our mother was ordered to attend as well as the rest of us. "Sparrow" in the Bible means any small bird: "Be not afraid. Are not two sparrows sold for a penny? Yet not one of them will fall to the ground apart from the will of your Father." Brown sparrows fly in a white sky. The sky may darken and turn to red. Listen for a song sung inside the hollow bones of their wings in flight.

Here is the second moment from which the master narrative's governing scene is constructed:

When I knew I had found my Savior I got right up in that meeting and told everybody so and since that time I have never been alone. I did not cast off the chains of slavery at the time of the surrender, they fell off at that camp meeting.

I diagrammed the battle of Antietam endlessly when I was thirteen (the year was 1963): a victory for the North—emancipation's needed opportunity—all the dead lying in Maryland. True virtue consists in consent to being in general.

Here is an event that connects the two of us: Upon leaving the Hospital for Special Surgery in New York City on July 13, 2008, after a routine check-up (I had had to have a hip replacement in the spring), I saw Donald Rumsfeld standing in the lobby. It was his notes and signature on the draft of a previous Office of Legal Counsel memorandum, written by others in 2002, authorizing torture, that your legal finding was intended officially to withdraw. I read your document, even with footnote 8, to require the arrest and trial for crimes against humanity of those at the highest levels of government who ordered torture in August 2002.

I saw no bodyguards protecting him. His wife, concerned and loving, hovered near. Nothing prevented me from action. What true speech do we have for the weather of our fear?

Your training in law and mine in history have been superb. Why did neither of us attempt to make a citizen's arrest? How else are we supposed to define the duty of true citizenship?

Once you have chosen your master narrative, commit it carefully to memory with vivid scenes that will allow you to bring your master narrative to conscious attention for reflective use under any circumstances whatsoever.

Second Day's Exercise (Historical Subject: George Anderson): Practice summoning and holding in mind the master narrative you have chosen. Develop as necessary the governing scene with which you bring it to mind. The object of a historical method is to make the present available for a virtuous action. Remember that the project of American history is life, liberty, and the pursuit of happiness.

At the end of each meditation address your words in imagination to an equal. Petition that person directly for understanding. This section of the method is called the Colloquy. Here is an example from my own second day's exercise:

Colloquy: I witness the governing scene of my master narrative with a child's eye: George Anderson did not feel any special resentment against the master; my voice grows softer still as I tell you of one episode from his life: "By and by, late in the afternoon, my brother did not cry out anymore, just swayed from side to side, side to side going lower all the time until he went down and did not come up again."

I have made these words into my own speech for another history in the New World. Do not think me presumptuous. I have no alternatives. We have whispering knowledge among us that Robert is the master's son. This knowledge has been acted upon but not given its emancipative historical form: a moment of reciprocated speech between equal historical selves.

Notes for a Love Song

Before pictures in the mind are worn away by inattention, they may be converted into the mental sounds of musical notes. This procedure is designed to preserve the capacity of the governing scene to create new understandings and put them into a rearranged reciprocity of words.

The first exercise of the method's complete cycle should be devoted to the goal of producing imagined sounds (timbre, pitch, duration, and volume) for individual notes. Melody will come easily once you have achieved the technical mastery behind the production of each note. With these notes and melodies together, we will imagine a New World reciprocity with which to live another history.

Directions on how to hear and reproduce the mental sound of my first note are given below. I have developed an easy notational system that I will now ask you to learn by heart.

The first musical note resulting from my practice of the second week's first exercise is written in the following way: I. I. i(a); i(b).

The first Roman numeral's position refers to the week's

historical subject. (A list of the four historical subjects of any complete cycle of this method's practice are to be written down on the first day of the first week. (See Table One, p. 33.)

The week of the first historical subject's meditations (this will be second week the first time through this method and the first week of the method's cycle thereafter) is given over to the master narrative itself. The notation for the first element of the sound of the first subject's first note is formally written as Roman numeral "I," accompanied (until familiarity with the rules of the method makes this no longer necessary) by the note's explication.

So, from the example of my own practice, in expanded form, the notation for the first element of the sound of my first note appears as: I. Historical Subject: George Anderson (Governing scene: "So they began to beat him early in the morning. . ." merging with "When I knew I had found my Savior I got right up in that meeting and told everybody so and since that time I have never been alone. I did not cast off the chains of slavery at the time of the surrender, they fell off at that camp meeting.").

The middle position and middle capital Roman numeral are reserved for the truth statement that informs the sound of the note being constructed. Again, the list of truth statements your method uses will have been written down during the first week in the spaces provided following the explanation of Table Two. (See p. 36.) It is crucial for the sake of fluency and ease of composition that these truth statements be memorized and refreshed daily as much as is necessary through silent recitation.

The middle position of my first mental note's transcription is correctly read as: I. Truth Statement: Every ruling minority needs to numb, and, if possible, to kill the time-sense of those whom it exploits by proposing a continuous present. This is the authoritarian secret of all methods of imprisonment.

The third position of the musical note's designation is reserved for, first, a lower case Roman numeral followed by the lower case Latin alphabet letter "a" and then for a second lower case Roman numeral followed by the lower case Latin alphabet letter "b." This position of the note's designation is reserved for the pair of Constructive Principles being used to create the sound of each note. In each case one positive and one negative principle are used together to generate the sound. Only one pair of principles is used to create the sound of any given note. It is best to restrict yourself to four pairs of constructive principles during any given month's meditative cycle. (See Table Three, pp.36-40.)

Again, the pairs of Constructive Principles you will be using in your own practice should be written down during the first week in the spaces provided on pages [page 40] of this manual.

Hold the results of your First Day's contemplation confirming your choice of a master narrative with the mental sound of the first musical note: *I. I. i(a); i(b).* This is difficult to accomplish at first but will come quite easily and naturally with regular practice once you have memorized the truth statements and constructive principles and they have become firmly lodged in your mind.

Obviously vivid, sometimes unbearable pictures must spring to mind as a result of employing this meditative technique. This cannot be avoided and should not be held to be an impediment or failing of any kind, caused either by a fault in the method or a weakness on the part of the practitioner. Indeed, it is the bringing of the terror of scenes, from whatever source, under the command of disciplined, expressive, auditory, communicative form that implies reciprocity and therefore the promise of forgiveness and relief.

Written out in its extended notational form, *I. I. i(a); i(b).*, the first mental note's sound, registering the immediacy of history as it appears in consciousness, can be represented as follows:

I. Historical Subject: George Anderson (Governing Scene: "So they began to beat him early in the morning. . . ." merging with "When I knew I had found my Savior I got right up in that meeting and told everybody so and since that time I have never been alone. I did not cast off the chains of slavery at the time of the surrender, they fell off at that camp meeting."

I. Truth Statement: Every ruling minority needs to numb, and, if possible, to kill the time-sense of those whom it exploits by proposing a continuous present. This is the authoritarian secret of all methods of imprisonment.

i(a). Constructive Principle (positive): The emancipative capacity of bourgeois literacy to instantiate the universal freedom of the autonomous individual as the transcendent secular project of modern history.

i(b). Constructive Principle (negative): The strategically administered historylessness of contemporary daily life: Empire's substitution of the promise of wealth for social justice as the basis of the consent of the governed.

Colloquy: I cannot improve upon the description in the Jesuit version of this method of the colloquy's purpose: "The colloquy is made by speaking exactly as one friend speaks to another, or as a servant speaks to a master, now asking him for a favor, now blaming himself for some misdeed, now making known his affairs to him, and seeking advice in them." At the end of most days' exercises you will be asked to address directly someone for whom you care a great deal. Once you have established the sound of the day's note, permit yourself to enter freely into a colloquy with any person of your choosing, imagined or real.

Colloquy for I. I. i(a); i(b): Eels in the sweet water's net—this Eastern Shore: the fresh smell of the stripped bark of the new ash post set in the yard yesterday by Mr. Vane. We own as much as we can hold—a stewardship wedded to a New World surveyor's eye. Authority is distant. Tell me what you see when you think of fathers killing sons. My master was a minister. He was a strict man who preached every Saturday and Sunday and on other days gave his attention to the farm. There is one subject of conversation of which he never tires. He is a devout Christian and his faith is beautiful. He can quote chapter after chapter from the Bible, and God is very real and very near to him. If our demands were not so extreme, there would be no need for musical sound.

Third Day's Exercise (Historical Subject: George Anderson): Begin by practicing again calling to mind your master narrative and its governing scene. After you have done this for the space of several minutes, create the mental sound of a second note for what you have just seen. Adjust the sound of the first subject's second note (timbre, pitch, duration, and volume) according to the promptings of the juxtaposition and simultaneous temporal overlay of the following elements from the three tables: *I. II. ii(a); ii(b)*.

Here, taken as an example from my own practice, is the sound of my first historical subject's (George Anderson) second note:

I. II. ii(a); ii(b).

Extended Notation:

I. Historical Subject: George Anderson (Governing scene: "So they began to beat him early in the morning . . . etc.," combined with "When I knew I had found my Savior . . . etc.")

II. Truth Statement: The most important principle of poetics is the structure of events, for tragedy is the mimesis not of persons but of life and action. Happiness and unhappiness consist in action and the goal is a certain kind of action and not a qualitative state. It is by virtue of character that persons have certain qualities, but it is by their actions that they are happy or the reverse.

ii(a). Constructive Principle (positive): It is both necessary and possible to live the one true history of your one true love. This is fidelity.

ii(b). Constructive Principle (negative): Under conditions of historylessness reciprocity must be improvised moment to moment.

Colloquy: This section is intimate spontaneous speech addressed in imagination to an equal. (The Colloquy should come at the end of each day's contemplation and should be engaged in without self-censorship or self-blame. It should be delivered as imagined accompaniment to the sound of the day's note. This will give your immediacy of speech a necessary reflective distance and allow you to think from a position where you are not. Leave time for the Colloquy each day no matter how busy your schedule. Generally it is best to allow twenty to forty minutes each day for the contemplative practice of a historical method. You will find yourself devoting more time to it as you progress.)

In the event you called it torture—in your mind, with

your voice, and in the pain and panic in your body. You had bravely decided you wanted access to experience to enable you to define the words of the statute. Then, by adding the footnote you included later, you declared torture legal when used on those we held within our control. Did you do so out of a sense of devotion to the duties of your office to support the executive branch—or did you do so as the result of a direct, illegal order? The jurisprudence created at Nuremberg ruled there was no justifiable defense for such an action—power is not truth and therefore cannot be law. Do we know now how to state the positive version of this truth and act on it without restraint?

I am the beneficiary of the order you enforced. I enjoy the pleasures of empire and did not act when I had the chance to make a citizen's arrest on July 13, 2008. I edited and helped write a war criminal's self-laudatory memoir. Every moment is forfeit in a history of absolute loss. If successful, practitioners of this method may choose a motto for their collective action to superimpose upon all the inscribed stones bearing the military command: *Ad majorem gloriam dei.*

> *Every moment forfeit/In this history of absolute loss:/I am valuable because she came back./If you see Leda before I do/Sing her this song so/She does not/choose another./I will do the same for you/If, while you are away,/I meet your one true love/ And you teach me the words. Refuse/Empire; create reciprocity/Among equal historical selves.*

Fourth Day's Exercise (Historical Subject: George Anderson): Memorize the eighth footnote of your December 30, 2004 legal finding: "While we have identified various disagreements with the August 2002 Memorandum, we have reviewed this Office's prior opinions addressing issues involving treatment of detainees and do not believe that any of their conclusions would be different under the standards set forth in this memorandum." What does this mean?

In the event, your footnote confirmed, instead of withdrew, torture as official policy approved in American law. Would you have signed this document if you had not been given a hand signal by which the torture you endured would be stopped immediately at the pleasure of your will? To how many bodies, lacking such control, was torture applied as a matter of justified legal procedure between 2002 and 2008 in pursuit of American happiness and within a rhetorical enforcement of perfected, exceptionalist history? When you and I take responsibility for what we have done, what narrative of purpose should we use?

I realize I commit here the fallacy of making you into a representative man. But isn't that what our training prepared us to do as a sign of our class's right to exercise stewardship and universal rule?

Hold the results of this exercise in mind with the imagined sound of the week's third note: *I. III. iii(a); iii(b).*

Extended notation: I. Historical Subject: George Anderson (Governing scene: "So they began . . . etc.," merging with "When I knew . . . etc."). III. Truth Statement: I would like to arrive at the point where I am able to grasp the essence of a certain place and time, compose the work, and play it on the spot naturally. iii(a). Constructive Principle (positive): The only serious philosophical question is what Eurydice saw when Orpheus looked back. What Eurydice saw when Orpheus looked back determines the worth of his song. iii(b). Constructive Principle (negative): Events under imperial rule unfold according to a technocratic logic of stochastic determination. The outcome of events gains unanswerable authority from the logic of their determination. Stochastics is that branch of statistical mathematics that concerns random sets of observations, each of which is plotted as a point on a separate distribution curve.

Colloquy (delivered to the accompaniment of the mental sound of the first historical subject's third note): Moment to moment our moral compass is overthrown by the violence by which we prosper. Knowledge is given back as spectacle that promises ecstasy but fuels the rage of unacknowledged dispossession. We took the same American history courses at Harvard. What logic or narrative of democracy now validates the conduct of our rule? What would happen if we gave each other the true results of a disciplined contemplative practice of the present as history?

When we worked on his book together, Fred Avery and I came up with a rhetorical shape for a narrative account of his years as Director of Central Intelligence between 1998 and 2005 with which we, the agency, and NCI were all happy: The conscientious family man keeping the country safe by all means necessary, making sure no secret, extra-legal violence was used that was not absolutely necessary—protecting all such knowledge from harming the reputation or moral resilience and resolve of the nation—protecting with adequate power and patriotic piety the innocent sources of American good faith—indulging as a necessary cost of democracy the contemptible, irresponsible criticism of dangerous ideologues with the assurance of vindication by a grateful posterity's enjoyment of unmatched American power and wealth. The book has sold nearly two hundred thousand copies. I could not resist the enjoyment of my contribution to this success.

Power's pleasures were written as self-sacrifice in the public interest. Devotion to family and country were written to suggest they entailed the burdens of atrocity in fighting savage wars a moral man could not refuse. Frederick Avery's strength and discipline, we implied, spared the ordinary citizen the moral consequences of dominion.

When I learned from Fred Avery what you had done, I knew I had to return to the moment of vision I had had at Mary Joscelyn's service a year before. I knew I needed to devise a formal method for living another history.

Fifth Day's Exercise: In the Jesuits' version of this method, the fifth day of the second week is given to the contemplation of Jesus' journey from Nazareth to the river Jordan to be baptized. I give you here the scene I use in my own practice on this day. If our meeting on June 19th is successful, I hope someday you will give me yours.

On the fifth day of the first historical subject's meditations, I assign myself the task of meditating upon the character (from the evidence provided by his choice of written words) of Marion C. MacRobert, the reporter who interviewed George Anderson in 1925. I have memorized these words to make his speech my own:

> He is George Anderson, colored, a former slave, whose records show him to be 108 years old. He lives with his daughter, Mrs. Fanny Coleman, who was a little girl when the Civil War ended, and whose grandchild, Cora Edna, a plump little kiddie with feet forever keeping time to some imaginary tune, is "Uncle George's" constant companion.

Uncle George is unable to walk because his poor old legs crumple up when he puts the weight of his feeble old body upon them, so that he spends the greater part of his time sitting on the side of his bed. But his eyes are bright and his memory very good. Now and then during a conversation his mind will wander off into by-paths and must be brought back sharply, but with careful handling he can tell a straightforward story of his youth and of the years before and after "the surrendah," as he speaks of the end of the Civil War.

Now attempt this contemplation of character using the mental sound of your own voice and using the words from something you have said or recently written as evidence. Attempt to discern from this exercise the relation of the speaker to the legal application of limitless force.

Hold in mind the results of this exercise with the imagined sound of the following note constructed from the method's three tables: *I. IV. iv(a); iv(b).*

Extended notation: I. Historical Subject: George Anderson (Governing scene: "So they began . . . etc.," combined with "When I knew I had found . . . etc."). IV. Truth Statement: Some discouragement, some faintness of heart at the new real future that replaces the imaginary, is not unusual, and we do not expect people to be deeply moved by what is not unusual. That element of tragedy which lies in the very fact of frequency, has not yet wrought itself into the coarse emotion of mankind; and perhaps our frames could hardly bear very much of it. If we had a keen vision and feeling of all ordinary human life, it would be like hearing the grass grow and the squirrel's heart beat and we should die of that roar which lies on the other side of silence. As it is, the quickest of us walk about well wadded with stupidity. iv(a). Constructive Principle (positive): Create or join with others to form a Society of Equal Historical Selves (SOEHS); iv(b). Constructive Principle (negative): Attend to the sound of voices behind the words of your thoughts filled with the reproach of all the anonymous, New World dead.

Colloquy to accompany the fourth note's sound: I will be proposing when we meet in person that we plan to travel to Fallujah together to talk to people there about what we have done. We gave ourselves the right to perpetrate collective punishment upon an entire city to be enjoyed as a pleasure without limit because we said a photograph of dishonored bodies of Americans offended us. I cannot tell if I mean my proposal to visit Fallujah together metaphorically or literally—my method attempts to make the two into a single form of knowledge as sometimes happens in dreams or visions. I want us to stand on the bridge where the mercenaries' bodies were hung and begin another history. People will say this can't be done. But you and I were educated for rule. Surely we can use the authority empire gives us to insist that after knowledge must come forgiveness. And after such forgiveness what knowledge can we afford to be without? Not even impunity is beyond the shape given it by the voices of all the anonymous dead.

Sixth Day's Exercise: Repeat, once in the morning, once in the afternoon, when possible, the fourth and fifth days' contemplations. (In my own practice these are: The memorization of the eighth footnote of your memorandum legally establishing torture as a legitimate instrument of American policy to be used at will by officers of the executive branch of the American government; and meditation upon a speaker's character from the perspective of that speaker's words concerning the limitless application of force.)

Hold the results of your contemplations during this exercise in mind with the imagined sound of the following note constructed from the following elements from the method's three tables: *I. V. i(a); i(b)*. Note: In imitation of functionalist principles of stochastic determination and the application of statistical mechanics to human command functions, the serial order of the application of the elements of the method's three tables in the construction of mental sounds for musical notes is strictly adhered to throughout these exercises. As illustrated here, therefore, the construction of the mental sound of the fifth note is accomplished by the application of the fifth truth statement (*Whenever events lose their independent value, an abstruse exegesis is born*), as you would expect, but then by the application of the first pair of Constructive Principles (*Emancipative capacity of bourgeois literacy and Historylessness*). This is because there are only four pairs of Constructive Principles in all so the next in the series after the fourth must be a return to the first in imitation of the temporal linearity of historical duration ("time's arrow"), despite the continued incidence and determining influence of cycles of repetition.

Extended notation: I. Historical Subject: George Anderson (Governing scene: "So they began to beat him early in the morning . . . etc.," combined with "When I knew I had found my Savior . . . etc.") V. Truth Statement: Whenever events lose their independent value, an abstruse exegesis is born. i(a). Constructive Principle (positive): The emancipative dimension of bourgeois literacy. i(b). Constructive Principle (negative): Contemporary historylessness.

Colloquy (delivered to the accompaniment of the first historical subject's fifth note): Midstream—there is nothing to lose—not even an angle of vision. How have we managed to attain such safety? Your one true love chooses you among all the rest. How does she discern your value among all the men pursuing her? I am valuable because she came back.

This method has taken me years to develop and assemble into a useable shape. Sometimes now I'm happy with it. When I recently separated from my wife of thirteen years, the method helped me know how to care for Lily, my teenage daughter. My method helps me attend to the beauty of Frears's music. I wouldn't be able to hear it accurately otherwise.

I will retire in due course. My official corporate leave from McClaren Books expires at the end of this year. I hope to be invited to serve for another term on the Frears Center's Board of Trustees.

All stories converge. All this because Owen Corliss refused to give me his equivalent scene when I came to the end of myself in that vision during the music at Mary Joscelyn's service. I'm confident I know the mistake I made and am determined not to repeat it. I'm determined there shall be no more inaction as the result of failures of historical narration.

Frears' music teaches that there is a politics of lyric behind each moment's breath to which words are never adequately accountable. This creates a politics of expressive presence that education appropriates for instrumental purposes. The promise of absolute possession in the New World had to be fulfilled before it could be abandoned. You will find other people standing there when you come to the end of yourself: Refuse empire; create reciprocity.

The flutist and composer, Charles Jason Frears, when he was twelve, watched his father dying of untreated stomach cancer. Every day he came home from school to find his father sitting in the middle of his bed surrounded by instruments—cornet, guitar, violin, and drum. When his father died, Frears stopped speaking for a year. He played his flute instead. When a musician who later played with him first heard Frears' sound on a recording, he was shocked to realize he was listening to music made from the sound of someone crying.

Frears' compositions often came to him first as words. When the music arrived, he discarded them. History as unbearable presence can take no other accurate, empirical form. A sparrow's freedom converges in New England's and Jamaica's unsponsored light. A psalm's praise for being that our training teaches us to mouth with confidence now lacks all conviction. Imagine the sound of a lyric creating a politics for refusing empire.

Seventh Day's Exercise: Juxtapose in the mind the governing scene with which you quickly bring to consciousness your master narrative and one of the photographs of the mercenaries' bodies hanging from Fallujah's bridge. You know the ones I mean. Devise a narrative with which these bodies are taken down, made whole, and laid beside the three thousand dead in the city we destroyed to revenge civilian self-knowledge of the limits and moral texture of impunity.

Hold the results of this exercise in your mind with the mental sound of the first historical subject's sixth note assembled from your method's three tables: I. VI. ii(a); ii(b).

Extended notation: I. Historical Subject: George Anderson (Governing scene: "So they began. . . ." etc.). VI. Truth Statement: When the whole world is a computer and all cultures are recorded on a single tribal drum, the fixed point of view of print culture will be irrelevant and impossible no matter how valuable. ii(a). Constructive Principle (positive): It is both necessary and possible to live the one true history of your one true love. ii(b). Constructive Principle (negative): Under conditions of empire, reciprocity among equals must be improvised moment-to-moment and dissolved in the immediate, managed violence of competitive interest and private advantage.

Colloquy (delivered to the accompaniment of the first historical subject's sixth note): This sound of a flute played inside the hollow bone of a sparrow's wing in flight. Are not two sparrows sold for a penny? You wrote in your memorandum legalizing torture: "Because the statute does not define 'severe,' we construe the term in accordance with its ordinary or natural meaning. The common understanding of the term 'torture' and the context in which the statute was enacted also inform our analysis. We have reviewed this Office's prior opinions addressing issues involving treatment of detainees and do not believe that any of their conclusions would be different under the standards set forth in this memorandum."

When you wrote these words, what images did you attach to them in your immediate thought?

Note: During most weeks of historical contemplation you will be composing the mental sounds of seven notes. Because the first day of the first historical subject's meditation is devoted to the choice of an overall master narrative and its confirmation without chance of revision, construction of the sound of particular notes does not begin until the second day of this week. This is why only six notes have been composed so far. If this creates a sense in the mind of an uncompleted musical scale, so much the better in that it shows that the mind is already constructing an architecture available for memory's reflection on lyric's spontaneous melodies.

THIRD WEEK

*Every moment forfeit in this history of absolute loss:
I am valuable because she came back. If you see
Leda before I do, sing her this song so she does not
choose another. I will do the same for you if, while
you are away, I meet your one true love and you
teach me the words.*

The goal of a historical method in our present is the disciplined dissolution of an imperial self in the interests of the possibilities of democracy. You and I have been taught speech for two sides of an American imperial coin: Roman peace like a desert and English jurisprudence on one and the narrative realism of an enlightened end to history on the other. "But when a long Train of Abuses and Usurpations, pursuing invariably the same Object, evinces a Design to reduce them under absolute Despotism, it is their Right, it is their Duty, to throw off such Government, and to provide new Guards for their future Security. Such is now the Necessity which constrains us to alter our former Systems of Government. For support, with a firm Reliance on the Protection of divine Providence, let us mutually pledge to each other our Lives, our Fortunes, and our sacred Honor."

The abundance of capitalism can be completed as either atrocity or the fulfillment of its promise of material freedom beyond the coercions and crimes of domination.

I once heard a historian of the Enlightenment, prating of his own commitment to empirical reason as the enemy of despotism, hurl from the academic podium the dictum that history happens only once and in only one way. He was making the case for the United States as the indispensable nation. From all things, one purpose, one empire, one happy ending—no matter what atrocities were unfolding.

Our foremost philosopher died from a smallpox vaccination before he could write what he announced as the great American book: *A History of the Work of Redemption in the New World.* He intended, he said, to hasten and beneficially affect (with the assistance of Divine grace) the fulfillment of God's plan by considering all parts of the grand scheme in their historical order. Scripture and event had never been made one through the practice of revealed religion until history and the work of redemption had been made one in experience. This logic of form produces the popular genre of personal narrative.

Grace redeemed time in New England through the enlivening word (past and future were fused on the page). Nothing was to intervene—not history or memory—between words and things. Geometry can be made to show that true virtue consists in consent to being in general.

In my own practice the historical subject of the third week is Derek Takes, Judith Takes and Charles Jason Frears' son. Derek was born January 31, 1965. Judith and Frears began an affair in the summer of 1963 when Judith was twenty-five and Frears was thirty-seven. (Jason Frears died suddenly in 1967 at the age of forty at the height of his creative powers.)

In the Jesuit version of this method the third week of contemplations treats the life of Jesus from the time he travels from Bethany to Jerusalem (this is during the day of the last supper) until his crucifixion as a criminal and his burial in the sepulcher by Joseph and Nicodemus in the presence of his mother. (Armed guards were posted by the authorities at the tomb to watch through the night to prevent Jesus' followers from robbing the grave and thus to fulfill the prophecies.)

First Day's Exercise: Choose someone you know to be the historical subject of your third week's practice of these exercises. Practice with the thought of someday telling that person that you once enlisted them in your mind in the project of living the present as history.

I have told Derek of my plan to develop this method and what his father's music means to me. For the past two years we have served together on the Board of Trustees of the new Frears center. (Its official name at the insistence of the university is The Charles Jason Frears Memorial American Music Archive and Performance Center at the University of Maryland—New Carrollton.)

Derek as historical subject did not appear clearly during my practice of these exercises despite my best efforts. His mother was my friend and colleague; his father's music produced this method; I saw him grow into manhood. My investments in his presence block the gates between word and vision. All visions must fail along the way if they are to succeed at all. History's great gift is time itself—an emptiness of contemplation untouched inside a note's duration by the logic of our class's preemptive strikes upon it. Words, it is said, will fill time at the end and make us whole in retrospect. Derek is not present here. The vision brightens. I reserve judgment and listen to his father's song.

Derek is both a musician and an educator overseeing

middle school social science curriculum development in the New Bern, North Carolina public schools. Derek has been generous in his encouragement of my attempt to use his father's art as model for a lyric rhetoric of historical presence.

Once you've chosen someone you know to be the historical subject for your contemplations during the method's second (third if you are just beginning) week, construct a governing scene by which to call your investment in that person's story to mind easily and vividly. (Many of this week's exercises will call upon you to juxtapose this governing scene with the governing scene you chose with which you bring immediately to mind your overall master historical narrative.)

Here is the background you will need to follow my own practice of this week's exercises. Derek is Judith and Charles Jason Frears's son. On the birth certificate from New Haven Hospital Judith gave Derek her own last name and gave him his father's last name for a middle one.

The governing scene I have constructed for Derek as the historical subject of my third week's contemplations is a composite one derived from two separate events. They became linked in my mind before I had time to question them. Neither is honorable. I would have them be different if I could. Historical vision must begin from where we find ourselves.

I give you this governing scene without hesitation in support of the request I am making that we meet in person when we are both in New Carrollton on June 19th:

I arrived at Yale Graduate School in the fall of 1976 to study early American history with Professor Charles Andrews Quick. I was twenty-seven. Judith Takes was two years ahead of me. She was writing her dissertation with Quick on the audience reception of early abolitionist rhetoric. She wanted, she told me, to try to relate levels of literacy to American self-understandings concerning the distinctiveness of American nationality and economic dependence upon slavery.

Judith was in her mid-thirties, having interrupted her academic career to raise Derek alone. His father was absent. She had financial support from her parents and the executors of the Frears estate. Frears' wife Corrine generously fulfilled the provisions Frears had asked her to make for Derek's upbringing just before he died.

I met Judith during a dinner for graduate students at Quick's house and we became friends. Judith was beautiful in a New England way I was used to. She had a beauty of reticence people remembered. (She was tall with the grace of the reed the heron stands next to at the head of the lake in early summer before the sun burns the morning mist away.)

I got the chance to know Derek slightly when he was a child. I once spent a whole day with him when he was eleven. (Judith was struggling to meet a deadline for a paper she was scheduled to deliver at a conference and accepted my offer to take him for a Saturday while she wrote.) As I remember it, Derek and I visited the Dinosaurs in the university's natural history museum and then took baseball gloves and a tennis ball and watched two softball teams play a pick-up game on the Yale playing fields off Dixwell Avenue.

Eventually, sometime in the mid-eighties, Judith got a full-time teaching job at Concord Community College. (We are still in touch, but we have not talked lately.)

The first element of the governing scene I use for this week's practice comes in a moment of mid-morning spring light. This must have been in 1983 or 1984. I was walking toward the green on Whitehall Street on my way to pick up music I had ordered when I was jolted by my sudden violent reaction to something I had just seen without knowing what it was at first.

In front of the music store (the shop's entrance door was

two or three steps below street level) I saw a tall laughing youth with long, curly, unkempt golden hair bending with the litheness of a just-discovered height to lay his head on a smiling woman's shoulder. She was looking up at him with a playful joy. I stood transfixed by an instant, limitless rage at what I had witnessed (American nationalism is made from the refusal to say accurately what it is to be white).

Of course what had registered before thought had been turned into speech in the mind was that who I was seeing were Judith and Derek. This American fact, and its refusal, of a white woman and her black son—their happiness—outshone the sun. The white possession of the self is untenable.

The second element of my governing scene for the second historical subject comes from the event in my life of which I am the most ashamed. Two days after the scene I had witnessed in front of the music store I attended a history conference in Lexington, Kentucky. I was delivering a paper on the last day on the invention in the early nineteenth century of an American national historical narrative.

The night of the first day of the conference I went to a strip club on a side street not far from my hotel. I drank whiskey and fell in love with one of the dancers. Her beauty struck (and seemed to me) beyond anything I had ever known. Her name was Jesse Bishop.

When I first saw Jesse Bishop, she was naked on a table in front of six white men sitting there around her. (I was at the bar.) The men's lust transfigured them. I heard crying in the room I couldn't see. The room seemed filled with it.

I thought I saw the men feel in her movements the truth of their own desire of which their fear deprived them and for whose sudden public display and knowledge, I thought their smiles and money said, they would never forgive her.

I thought I saw her answer their money with the abandon

of her contempt. She was very young. Her gaze was like an instrument and felt fluent as a touch.

When the six men left, I paid her to dance for me as long as I could. Although it was against the rules, she allowed me to drive her home.

While she sat with me between dances, the bartender handed her a corded phone. It was her six-year-old son who couldn't sleep. His name was Robert. Jesse said Robert was allowed to call her twice a night if he couldn't sleep but no more than that no matter what. (There was no one Jesse could afford to pay to stay with Robert the hours that she worked.)

When, near dawn, we reached the driveway of her small home in a new development on the outskirts of Lexington (we had driven in my rented car), I asked if I could come in. I said I wanted to see Robert sleeping. She said she must be crazy, but she let me. There in a narrow child's bed I saw a child's untethered breathing—and realized it was a discipline I had never learned and didn't know how to steal.

I took my leave of her and went back to my hotel. The next afternoon (the day before my presentation), after many hours of driving, I found her house again, and walked up to her door. I did not have the courage—though I knew I had found my one true love—to knock. There was no bell.

The second element of my governing scene for the method's second historical subject is myself watching Jesse dancing on the table in Lexington, Kentucky to the accompaniment of the lust of seven white men.

You wrote in the legal finding you signed in December of 2004, "We have reviewed this Office's prior opinions addressing issues involving treatment of detainees and do not believe that any of their conclusions would be different under the standards set forth in this memorandum."

While pretending to withdraw the previous August 2002 opinion's findings (when did you realize you had failed at accomplishing this?), your signature made legal and exempted from prosecution the perpetrators of the actions described in the following document granting the executive branch permission to commit war crimes:

> You would like to place Zubaydah in a cramped confinement box with an insect. You have informed us that he appears to have a fear of insects. In particular, you would like to tell Zubaydah that you intend to place a stinging insect into the box with him. . . . Finally, you would like to use a technique called the "waterboard." In this procedure, the individual is bound securely to an inclined bench, which is approximately four feet by seven feet. The individual's feet are generally elevated. A cloth is placed over the forehead and eyes. Water is then applied to the cloth in a controlled manner. As this is done, the cloth is lowered until it covers both the nose and mouth. Once the cloth is saturated and completely covers the mouth and nose, air flow is slightly restricted for 20 to 40 seconds due to the presence of the cloth. This causes an increase in carbon dioxide level in the individual's blood. This increase in the carbon dioxide level stimulates increased effort to breath. This effort plus the cloth produces the perception of "suffocation and incipient panic," i.e., the perception of drowning. The individual does not breathe any water into his lungs. During those 20 to 40

seconds, water is continuously applied from a height of twelve to twenty-four inches. After this period, the cloth is lifted, and the individual is allowed to breathe unimpeded for three or four full breaths. The sensation of drowning is immediately relieved by the removal of the cloth. The procedure may then be repeated. The water is usually applied from a canteen cup or small watering can with a spout. You have orally informed us that this procedure triggers an automatic physiological sensation of drowning that the individual cannot control even through he may be aware that he is in fact not drowning. You have also orally informed us that it is likely that this procedure would not last more than 20 minutes in any one application.

Note: Here is how an instructor who oversaw hundreds of waterboarding sessions and underwent the experience himself explained to a reporter his objection to descriptions in the press of it as "simulated drowning":

"It's not simulated anything. It's slow-motion suffocation with enough time to contemplate the inevitability of blackout and expiration—usually the person goes into hysterics on the board. You can feel every drop. Every drop. You start to panic. And as you panic, you start gasping, and as you gasp, your gag reflex is overridden by water. And then you start to choke, and then you start to drown more. Because the water doesn't stop until the interrogator wants to ask you a question. And then, for that second, the water will continue, and you'll get a second to puke and spit up everything that you have, and then you'll have an opportunity to determine whether you're willing to continue with the process. Our waterboarders are professional. When the water hits you, you think, 'Oh shit, this is a whole new level of Bad.'" Make history a discipline for thinking from a place you are not.

George W. Bush, Richard Cheney, and Donald Rumsfeld requested and authorized these acts to be committed on the bodies of our enemies on behalf of the American people. Alberto Gonzales, David Addington, Jim Haynes, John Yoo, Jay Bybee, Douglas Feith and you, officers of the court and trained counselors of law, sworn to uphold signed treaties and statute laws against acts of torture, wrote binding legal opinions declaring these acts of torture legal when committed for purposes of guarding the security of the American state. Whenever any Form of Government becomes destructive of these Ends, it is the Right of the People to alter or to abolish it, and to institute new Government, laying its Foundation on such Principles, and organizing its Powers in such Form, as to them shall seem most likely to effect their Safety and Happiness. Prudence, . . .

Hold the results of the first day's exercise in mind with the mental sound of the musical note constructed from the following elements from the method's three tables: *II. I. i(a); i(b)*. (Again, the first day's meditative exercise during the week devoted to this method's second historical subject is to select someone you know and develop a governing scene with which to know them in history. Conduct your practice so that you will be able to tell them someday that you made this imaginative use of their presence.)

Extended notation taken from my practice of this exercise: II. Historical Subject: Derek Takes (Governing scene: Derek bending gracefully to place his head playfully on his mother's shoulder outside a music store on a New Haven street in

1982 merging with Jesse Bishop dancing naked on a table in front of six white men in a strip club in Lexington, Kentucky in the spring of 1982). I. Truth Statement: Every ruling minority needs to numb, and, if possible, to kill the time-sense of those whom it exploits by proposing a continuous present. This is the authoritarian secret of all methods of imprisonment. i(a). Constructive Principle (positive): The emancipative dimension of bourgeois literacy creates a sphere of disciplined imaginative freedom beyond the coercions of the marketplace. Universal print literacy as an Enlightenment goal implies a politics of lyric reciprocity—never fully applied in practice—contradicting the logic of accumulation by which contemporary capitalism operates. ii(b). Constructive Principle (negative): Historylessness prevents the construction of narratives of value and necessity in which abundance and the general welfare meet.

Colloquy (delivered to the accompaniment of the second subject's first note): Fathers killing sons. My father is gone now; I memorize what Marion C. MacRobert wrote. Mother too was unable to stand by herself in the presence of what had been done. Everything is owned.

Dear Derek,

You are the historical subject I could not see—your voice isn't here on the page though I have tried to hear it. I am jealous. You are the person I cannot be. Absence will have to do instead as an engine of narrative—some speech for another history. My condition is no different, I believe, from that of anyone else, although I have no direct proof of this. So much eye witness testimony has been suppressed that this proposition is impossible to test.

Law does not extend beyond the marchlands. Universalism shimmers distantly. My father did not oppose his father and did what he was told: too often. No approval came. His father came back from France in 1918, his character unrecognizable. My father's cousins told me this. My father was much honored for his learning and his contributions to humanism. Nothing was done. My mother slept under the eaves of her in-laws' money and continuously mourned losses she had not earned.

My father was a minister and a strict man. He believed in the Biblical rhythms of King James and championed a naturalist's plain style to communicate vision. Are not two sparrows sold for a farthing? and one of them shall not fall on the ground without your Father. / Fear ye not therefore, ye are of more value than many sparrows. I will not fail my daughter.

We are our fathers' sons. I hope "Light Years"—both music and lyrics—will bring us closer. It was your parents' song. And Leda will sing it in June. I see you leaning in light and your mother smiling. I believe that narrative techniques of discontinuity may be used as structures of consent.

I look forward to serving with you on the board of the archive and performance center built in your father's honor. We will be each other's allies, I trust and hope. I was your mother's friend and now study your father's art as if it were a discipline that could save my life. I realize you may be used to this.

I'm glad your mother spoke well of me and my ideas about American history and Protestant redeemed time. We used to joke about the virtue of limitless New World possession and seventeenth-century enclosures west of Suffolk and Northamptonshire. I remember telling you as a boy of Captain Pouch, the tinker who told his followers God would protect him and those with him who believed in their revolt with what he had in his large satchel. When they captured and killed him, the gentry claimed they opened it and found it full of green cheese. This is the way the encyclopedia now says it: "The rebels were indicted with High Treason and several were executed, including Captain Pouch, who was 'made exemplary.'"

History is a discipline with which to dissolve an imperial self. I have begun to practice it again by asking to meet with David Kallen on June 19th.

Yours sincerely,
Theo Fales

Second Day's Exercise: In your action you were brave beyond what anyone in your position had done in years. You sought to know the meaning of torture voluntarily through your own body's pain so that you could call it by its name. The eighth footnote of your legal finding then revoked the main text's finding of illegality and granted immunity from prosecution for war crimes to the president, vice-president, attorney general, secretary of defense, director of intelligence, and all their attorneys (among whom it is necessary to include yourself). Through you, torture was a policy chosen legally by U.S. citizens in 2002 and 2004 with which to realize the general will.

On this second day of meditation on the second historical subject, compose in your mind a narrative of democracy in which the U.S. state is the means of accomplishing justice. Our declaration of the ends of government and history—the universal rights of citizens—must be lived as more than ideology. Choose a story illustrating this necessity during this exercise.

Hold in mind the results of this exercise with the mental sound of the musical note constructed from the following elements of the method's three tables: *II. II. ii(a); ii(b).*

Extended notation: II. Historical Subject: Derek Takes (Governing scene: Derek bends down and playfully places his head on his smiling mother's shoulder. This scene gives way to and merges with the image of Jesse Bishop in a strip club in Lexington, Kentucky dancing naked in front of six white men). II. Truth Statement: The most important of these things is the structure of events, for tragedy is the mimesis not of persons but of life and action. Happiness and unhappiness consist in action and the goal is a certain kind of action and not a qualitative state. It is by virtue of character that persons have certain qualities, but it is through their actions that they are happy or the reverse. ii(a). Constructive Principle (positive): It is both possible and necessary to live the true history of your one true love. ii(b). Constructive principle (negative): Within structures of complicity, reciprocity must be improvised moment-to-moment each day. This is made difficult by the pleasures and rewards of benefitting from atrocity.

Colloquy (delivered to the accompaniment of the second note of the method's second historical subject): Liberalism's techniques of freedom as absolute possession made modern slavery possible. I am valuable because she came back.

I am valuable because a woman came back to see who I had become when I was four. I wrote one letter to Jesse Bishop. In it I asked about Robert. I never heard anything back.

Why did you sign the legal document making torture legal while claiming it was abhorrent both to American law and values and to international norms? Why do I not act more bravely to undo the results or what you wrote? How are either of us now to live the one true history of his one true love?

Third Day's Exercise: The goal throughout the practice of these exercises is to connect image, word, and act in a sequence with which to refuse empire and create reciprocity. The goal is to create some speech for the present as history. In the Jesuit version of this method, you are asked on the third day of the second subject's practice to remember Peter with a sword cutting off the ear of the high priest's servant. Jesus heals him: all failed acts can be rectified once narratives of transcendence are effectively in place in daily life. Events happen only once and in only one way. This is dogma and the basis for narrating historical justice. Whenever any Form of Government becomes destructive of these Ends it is the Right of the People to alter or to abolish it, and to institute new Government, laying its Foundation on such Principles and organizing its Powers in such Form, as to them shall seem most likely to effect their Safety and Happiness.

Law did not extend beyond the marchlands to native inhabitants and strangers whose lives were already forfeit. Everything in the New World could be possessed (this was our discovery). Incorporate this truth within a narrative principle chronicling events among equal historical selves.

From the Enlightenment principles of autonomy, community (formed on the basis of family love), and cultivation (through education) emerges the concept of a universal humanity (beginning to resonate with attributes like "pure" and "common") that opens onto an inner realm of freedom (operating by its own laws) without any extrinsic purposes whatsoever. Having created the notes of New World reciprocity, composed the music, and performed it naturally, ask your one true love to answer you from safe inside the common place you've made.

After my direct vision during the music at Mary Joscelyn's

funeral service, I found my one true love by acting on desire.

On July 13, 2008 I encountered Donald Rumsfeld at ease and unguarded in a public place and I did nothing. I cannot plead ignorance or any slackness in the discipline with which I practice this method.

In the event you were able to act and I was not. I gave a rhetorical shape to Fred Avery's memoir (I still consider him a friend) and attended the ceremony at which he received the Presidential Medal of Freedom. Barring another history, the rhetorical shape I gave to Fred Avery for his narrative of his years as the director of the CIA between 1997 and 2004 makes forgiveness meaningless.

I spend my days now sorting through Judith's papers, practicing this method, creating the notes of reciprocity it makes possible.

Hold in mind the results of this exercise's contemplations with the mental sound of the second subject's third note constructed from the combination of the following elements from the method's three tables: *II. III. iii(a); iii(b)*. (Remember that the task of this exercise is to apply to yourself the discovery in the New World that law beyond the marchlands did not apply to natives or strangers; order's logic then concludes that it lies in the general interest of human kind that everything can be owned.)

Extended notation: II. Historical Subject: Derek Takes (Governing scene: Derek gracefully bends towards his mother and places his head upon her shoulder. This moment gives way to the image of Jesse Bishop's unforgiving beauty as she dances on a table in a strip club in front of six white men. She braids their lust with their loss and cowardice and makes possession drunken and a portrait of the visible.). III. Truth Statement:

I would like to arrive at the point where I am able to grasp the essence of a certain place and time, compose the work, and play it on the spot naturally. iii(a). Constructive Principle (positive): The only serious philosophical question is the question of what Eurydice saw when Orpheus looked back. What she sees in his face determines the worth of his song. Orpheus sang to make epic accountable to lyric's sudden politics of light's immediacy—words and notes for what an event means or meant to someone privately—to you, to me. His voice wakes the weightlessness of stones in flight and makes love available for thought. "If I return to life for you, an instrumentalism of form will triumph over what the dead are murmuring." iii(b). Constructive Principle (negative): Empire replaces history with the stochastic management of the advantage secured through the application of unlimited force. Words fail to mean themselves. "Torture is abhorrent both to American law and values and to international norms." "While we have identified various disagreements with the August 2002 Memorandum, we have reviewed this Office's prior opinions addressing issues involving treatment of detainees and do not believe that any of their conclusions would be different under the standards set forth in this memorandum." Stochastics is that branch of statistical mathematics that concerns random sets of observations, each plotted as a point on an independent distribution curve. Narration establishes the redemptive logic of limitless force. Spectacle enforces complicity with empire. Complicity with torturers demands a lyrical politics of absolute loss.

Fourth Day's Exercise: Decide upon a valued quality possessed by your second historical subject's character. Show it in action by constructing a governing scene of democratic reciprocity. I failed to knock on Jesse and Robert's door the day after I drove Jesse home. The CIA destroyed the video recordings it had made for instructional purposes of the interrogations of high-value detainees. Frederick Avery made it a condition of the publication of his memoir by McClaren Books and NCI that the illegal destruction of this evidence not be mentioned in his memoir. I made no objections to this condition of publication nor did I include its meaning in the rhetorical shape I gave Fred Avery's first-person sincerity.

The quality I chose for Derek is his sympathy, after what his mother told him, for his father as a boy coming home from school to stand in front of Derek's dying grandfather sitting in the middle of his unmade bed surrounded by instruments (drum, cornet, violin, guitar). The moment of reciprocity I choose is Derek's decision to use the discipline he knew from his father's playing to build a school.

Hold the results of this exercise's contemplation in your mind with the mental sound of the second subject's fourth note. Construct this note by combining the following elements from the method's three tables: *II. IV. iv(a); iv(b)*.

Extended notation from my practice: II. Historical Subject: Derek Takes (Governing scene: Derek bends down towards his mother's smiling face. This scene gives way and merges with the image of Jesse Bishop dancing in front of six white men.). IV. Truth Statement: Some discouragement, some faintness of heart at the new real future that replaces the imaginary, is not unusual, and we do not expect people to be deeply moved by what is not unusual. That element of tragedy which lies in the very fact of frequency, has not yet wrought itself into the coarse emotion of mankind; and perhaps our frames could hardly bear very much of it. If we had a keen vision and feeling of all ordinary human life, it would be like hearing the grass grow and the squirrel's heart beat and we should die of that roar which lies on the other side of silence. As it is, the quickest of us walk about well wadded with stupidity. iv(a). Constructive Principle (positive): Create or join a society of equal historical selves (SOEHS). iv(b). Constructive Principle (negative): During the narration of history of any kind, be sure to attend to the sound of reproach in the voices of all the anonymous dead.

Colloquy (delivered defensively from inside the lost entitlement to absolute possession to the accompaniment of the second subject's fourth note): This white page—this immediacy. When you receive my phone call after having read and begun to practice this method for yourself, remember that I am valuable because she came back. (I learned from my mother's diary that the woman in my vision, standing in the doorway of my parents' apartment in New Haven, was, in the event, Melisande Chandless, a Jamaican nurse who cared for me as an infant when my mother couldn't take care of her newborn for the first thirteen weeks of its life. (My mother wrote in her diary that she turned to the wall and would not speak when her baby was offered her to hold.) She was mourning a first child who had died nine months before this new birth. She wrote that she couldn't bear the sight of another thing she would care for and fail. Art, she said, was the only thing that could make duration valuable. When narrating history of any kind, be sure to give your words, as much as you can, their local colors and sounds.

Fifth Day's Exercise: Narrate the moment you first decided to practice the present as history. For me I think it came early when I saw in the radiance of her face from behind my mother's skirt that I was valuable and worthy of her question. (I knew my mother would not let her through the door.) This happened when I was four and then again in my vision as I listened to the music at Mary Joscelyn's funeral. Words are sound and vision before they're written forms—open not just to interpretation but also to embodiment. Nevertheless, I know now few really listen to this music.

Hold in your mind the results of this exercise's meditations with the mental sound of the second subject's fifth note. Construct this note by combining the following elements from the method's three tables: *II. V. i(a); i(b)*. (The task of the exercise is to narrate the decision to experience the present moment as a historical one. History is a discipline with which to think from a place you are not.)

Extended notation from my practice: II. Historical Subject: Derek Takes (Governing scene: Derek bends towards his mother on a New Haven Street giving way to an image of Jesse Bishop's beauty turning time into event in front of six white men). V. Truth Statement: Whenever events lose their independent value an abstruse exegesis is born. i(a). Constructive Principle (positive): Reciprocity as a communicative ideal stems from the Enlightenment tradition of bourgeois literacy. i(b). Constructive Principle (negative): Historylessness, when enforced by a managerial ethos of administering the coercions of empire, creates despair.

Colloquy: It does no good to be too hard on yourself when considering the facts of our complicity. Most of us lack your bravery and the competence with which you accomplished (and, I assume, still accomplish) your tasks.

Sixth Day's Exercise: Place the moment of your decision to know the present as history within the governing scene of the master narrative you have chosen for practicing this method. For me this means joining what I saw during the music at Mary Joscelyn's service with the narrative of the life of George Anderson published in the Trenton *State Gazette* on April 6, 1925. Do not be afraid. Music accompanies unjust narrative. Remember what Marion MacRobert says of George Anderson: "He can quote chapter after chapter from the Bible, and God is very real and very near to him." What Eurydice saw in Orpheus's face ensures words' opening onto common speech to create an unformed future out of others' experience. Refuse empire; create reciprocity.

Hold the results of this day's meditation in your mind again with the mental sound of the second subject's sixth note constructed from the following elements from the method's three tables: *II. VI. ii(a); ii(b).* (Remember that the task of the exercise is to juxtapose the decision to live in the present as history and the governing scene of your master narrative.)

Extended notation from my own practice: II. Historical Subject: Derek Takes (Governing scene: Derek bends towards his mother. This picture gives way to and merges with an image of Jesse Bishop dancing her beauty in front of men). VI. Truth Statement: When the whole world is a computer and all cultures are recorded on a single tribal drum, the fixed point of view of print culture will be irrelevant and impossible no matter how valuable. ii(a). Constructive Principle (positive): It is both necessary and possible to live the one true history of your one true love. ii(b). Constructive Principle (negative): Reciprocity, under conditions of empire, must be improvised moment-to-moment. Every moment is forfeit in a history based on principles of limitless possession and absolute loss.

Colloquy delivered to the accompaniment of the second subject's sixth note: In New York State, in order to effect a citizen's arrest a person may use such physical force as is justifiable pursuant to subdivision four of section 35.30 of the penal law. Once the suspect has been taken into custody, it is the citizen's responsibility to deliver the suspect to the proper authorities in a timely fashion. I failed to obey this law on July 13, 2008 when I was in the presence of and in a position to apprehend an unprotected war criminal.

Seventh Day's Exercise: Construct an event in your mind in which your second historical subject's governing scene is interrupted by your need to declare your one true love. Sing a love song in imperial time. I never knocked on Jesse Bishop's door. When the Special Forces trainers were torturing you at Fort Bragg, did you imagine calling out to your one true love? Have the results of this exercise in readiness for the next time you are asked to affirm the link between American freedom and absolute possession.

Hold in your mind the results of your second subject's seventh contemplation with the mental sound of the note constructed from the following elements from the method's three tables: *II.VII. iii(a); iii(b).* (Remember that the task of the exercise is to sing a love song from the midst of a historical method's governing scene.)

Extended notation taken from my own practice: II. Historical Subject: Derek Takes (Governing scene: Derek bends down in New Haven morning light in front of a music store to rest his head playfully on his mother's shoulder. This scene merges with the picture of Jesse Bishop's beauty danced in front of men in Lexington, Kentucky in 1982 while the music is playing.). VII. Truth Statement: At first I was afraid. This familiar music demanded action of the kind of which I was incapable, and yet, had I lingered there beneath the surface I might have attempted to act. Nevertheless, I know now that few really listen to this music. iii(a). Constructive Principle (positive): The only important philosophical question is the question of what Eurydice saw when Orpheus looked back. iii(b). Constructive Principle (negative): The stochastic character of contemporary historical time makes the truthful narration of a historical subject's one true love uncertain and open to misuse even when properly framed as a matter of legitimate public concern. The problem of historical narration can be restated more formally in the following historical gloss Wikipedia gives to the term "stochastic":

> Any kind of time development (be it deterministic or essentially probabilistic) which is analyzable in terms of probability deserves the name of stochastic process. In the 1950s stochastic methods were used at Los Alamos for early work relating to the development of the hydorgen bomb, and became popularized in the fields of physics, physica chemistry, and operations research. The Rand Corporation and the U.S. Air Force were two of the major organizations responsible for funding and disseminating information on stochastic methods during this time, and they began to find a wide application in many different fields. Stochastic processes can

be used in music to compose a fixed piece or can be produced in performance. Stochastic social science theory is similar to systems theory in that events are interactions of systems, although with a marked emphasis on unconscious processes. The event creates its own conditions of possibility, rendering it unpredictable if simply for the amount of variables involved. Stochastic social science theory can be seen as an elaboration of a kind of 'third axis' in which to situate human behavior alongside the traditional 'nature vs. nurture' opposition.

Colloquy delivered to the accompaniment of the second subject's seventh note (I recite to you from memory the following words from the Trenton State Gazette article from April 6, 1925 written by Marion MacRobert):

> Uncle George is unable to walk because his poor old legs crumple up when he puts the weight of his feeble old body upon them so that he spends the greater part of his time sitting on the side of his bed. But his eyes are bright and his memory very good. Now and then during a conversation his mind will wander off into by-paths and must be brought back sharply, but with careful handling he can tell a straightforward story of his youth and of the years before and after "the surrendah," as he speaks of the end of the Civil War.

All stories of history that are to be called true deserve careful handling. Please send me, when you can, words you have chosen with which to memorize and hold onto the sounds of your master narrative, and I promise to try to make them my own, applying the arts of memory.

Derek's history is not here. (Our failures of representation make valuable self-portraits.) Let that be my excuse for including this week's improperly executed exercises here. In the sound of this seventh note let the dissonances stand out. I will do everything I can to establish, with your firm's help, Derek's entitlement as Judith Takes's heir to a share of the royalties from "Light Years."

I am valuable because she came back. What Eurydice sees in the need in Orpheus's eyes establishes the worth of his song. Her action opens a place only the living can fill. I hope we've both practiced this method and will agree to speak to the people we imagine gathering beneath the mercenaries' bodies swaying from Fallujah's bridge. From these actions we may be able to create historical speech for what we have done in the New World.

FOURTH WEEK

Do you tell yourself our superiority derives from our talents or from our legitimate exercise of immediate rule?

Our wars are not declared. The events resulting from the force our empire requires are not admissible evidence against us. It's true our frames could hardly bear very much of it. This is how republics end.

In this first cycle of this method's practice, the fourth week is reserved for the third historical subject. Choose it well. In subsequent cycles, the fourth week's exercises will be devoted to the practitioner himself as historical subject—to autobiography as self-help—a practical, political guide. During this first cycle, the last two days of your practice may be allotted to the task of beginning to compose musical notes for yourself as historical subject speaking in the first person. But for most, these last two days of the first cycle are better spent reviewing and securing in memory the method's tables of rules.

The object, when it comes to the fourth week of subsequent cycles, is to dissolve the imperial self and to trust those you find standing at the end of your vision.

In my own practice of this first cycle only, I chose Judith

Takes as my historical subject for the fourth week. Again I use a governing scene assembled as a composite made from two moments. The first merges and then gives way to the second in each exercise's actual practice. It is perfectly acceptable to use moments derived from your reading for your governing scenes rather than actual events. The goal is interpretive immediacy and perfect union between words and things, not legal standards of proof.

For the first moment of my third subject's governing scene I use a mental picture of a young woman listening to a young man speaking publicly. He is narrating his experience as a child entering history's literate clarity through what he calls "the bloodstained gates of slavery." This moment occurs on a New England summer evening in a public meeting hall on Nantucket Island. The year is 1841. The second moment of my third subject's governing scene comes from Judith's account to me of the moment she and Jason Frears fell in love. She had gone to hear him play in Greenwich Village club on his birthday. This was in early September of 1963.

Remember that the goal of this method is responsible immediacy for historical thought. These exercises are intended to help rid us of our attachments to empire and undo the consequences of historylessness. (American exceptionalism is not exceptional.)

In philosophy immediacy is an inference drawn from a single premise and therefore arrived at without the intervention of a middle term. Immediate knowledge is the knowledge of self-evidence. We hold these truths.

At Nuremberg it was established as legal doctrine that immoral laws could not make crimes against humanity immune from prosecution. The urgency of universal justice, given the destructive powers unleashed by modernity, is simply too great. Justice within modernity is understood to mean universal entitlement to individual freedom within a society of equal historical selves. This is conservative legal doctrine—not radicalism. All our Harvard training can be marshaled to prove that this is true. Or were we also being trained to overturn doctrine according to the necessity of maintaining order no matter how extreme the injustice of the event? Were we being trained to demonstrate, as part of the legibility of order, the impunity of our election? What is the appropriate citizen response, knowing what we know, to the president's statement to the nation delivered on July 5, 2004 that "Freedom from torture is an inalienable human right?"

In August of 2002 and again in late December of 2004, under the color of law and with the protection of the document you wrote and signed, the United States became the first nation to formally authorize the violation of the Geneva Conventions against torture and war crimes. There are no exceptions to the constraints placed by law upon acts of government officials under Common Article 3—not even immediate necessity, or national security. This article states that the following acts are prohibited under all circumstances: "Violence to life and person, in particular murder of all kinds, mutilation, cruel treatment and torture; outrages upon personal dignity, in particular humiliating and degrading treatment; and the carrying out of executions without previous judgment pronounced by a regularly constituted court, affording all the judicial guarantees which are recognized as indispensable by civilized peoples." The person who violates Common Article 3 is an international outlaw, liable to prosecution under universal jurisdiction.

"Immediate" in the seventeenth century, could be used as a noun that referred to the person who was the recipient of an urgent, spontaneous act of sacred communication, especially if he was a faithful believer, as in: "Christ is speedy, and swift as a roe, especially in his *immediates.*"

You and I were trained for the same pleasures and responsibilities. The second moment of the governing scene for the third subject's exercises is an image of Judith approaching Jason Frears as he is about to take a break during a performance at Greenwich Village jazz club in 1963. (It was his birthday and he was in the middle of a five-day booking.) Judith is saying, "I've brought you something for your birthday," and Frears, a married man, laughs gently answering, "You've brought me you."

Here is the first moment of the third subject's governing scene. A young married man is speaking, remembering himself as a six-year-old boy seeing for the first time a slave being whipped. He is watching his aunt—his mother's sister—being suspended, half naked, from an iron hook secured in a ceiling joist of an out-building by his master's overseer. She is to be whipped for his rage and pleasure. In the meeting hall the handsome man is speaking as if, for the first time, his voice is experiencing the limitlessness of possession in the New World. He is saying out loud what he remembers seeing as a child: "He would whip her to make her scream and whip her to make her hush. It was the bloodstained gate, the entrance to the hell of slavery through which I was about to pass. It was a most terrible spectacle. I wish I could commit to paper the feelings with which I beheld it."

When he comes to write the words of this speech down a year later, this is how he describes what happened:

> Her arms were stretched up at their full length, so that she stood upon the ends of her toes. He then said to her, "Now, you damned bitch, I'll learn you how to disobey my orders!"and after rolling up his sleeves, he commenced to lay

on the heavy cowskin, and soon the warm, red blood (amid heart-rending shrieks from her, and horrid oaths from him) came dripping to the floor. I was so terrified and horror-stricken at the sight, that I hid in a closet, and dared not venture out till long after the bloody transaction was over. I expected it would be my turn next. It was all new to me. I had never seen any thing like it before. I had always lived with my grand-mother on the outskirts of the plantation, where she was put to raise the children of the younger women. I had therefore been, until now, out of the way of the bloody scenes that often occurred on the plantation.

From what I know of Judith's work on the audiences of the early abolitionists, I know she imagined herself in the audience as a young New England Protestant woman, nine-teen or twenty, listening to a man speaking in public for the first time of his childhood vision of slavery. She told me she imagined the girl imagining herself as the master's daughter and speaker's playmate hiding in the closet with him. The girl listening, Judith said, was to be understood as a good student of New World New England light: The bloodstained gate was to be understood as history from the perspective of Apocalypse without an intermediary.

On the morning of June 19th, before the ceremonies, I will be speaking to the board of trustees on behalf of NCI and will announce the company's commitment to provide the seed capital to establish an operating endowment for the just-completed Charles Jason Frears Memorial American Music Archive and Performance Center at the University of Maryland—New Carrollton.

Another speaker, later in the day, will be announcing the discovery—I and others made it while going through Judith's papers at Derek's request—of lyrics in Judith's handwriting for Jason Frears's signature composition, "Light Years."

I have temporarily removed that original document from the archive. These lyrics were thought to have been lost. I will take responsibility for its safe keeping until its commercial value can be determined. It appears to me clear that Judith's estate is entitled as co-owner of copyright in the work and to a share of back royalties. These might amount to a considerable sum. I will turn the document over to the law firm that handles this matter on behalf of Derek and Judith's estate. I am recommending that Derek and his advisers consult you.

Last month I heard Leda sing "Light Years" in Toronto for her audition to be the artist in residence at the Frears Center this coming academic year. (She sang it in an arrangement she'd made of it as a melody without words scored for voice and flute.) When I heard and saw her singing, I knew I had found my one true love. From that moment I knew I was free to act on my desire.

I have declared my love to Leda. I was able to do so because of my practice of this method. From this experience I have learned to trust my method. That is why I now send you this letter.

My daughter, Lily Fales, will be at the dedication ceremonies on June 19th to hear me speak and to hear Leda sing. She is fourteen. I look forward to introducing you to her and likewise would be pleased to meet any members of your family who will be attending.

First Day's Exercise: In the Jesuits' version of this method, the fourth week is reserved for the events that establish the meaning of history by anticipating, prefiguring, and thereby enabling as historical event, its end: "Behold, I come quickly; and my reward is with me." I have loved and made a lie.

Using the governing scene you have constructed for the third subject's exercises, construct arguments your one true love will adopt as her own to refuse to obey illegitimate orders of the imperial state. True virtue consists in consent to being in general. Governments derive their just powers from the consent of the governed.

When you align the historical master narrative you have chosen with the scene of the bloodstained gate, what narrative of justice now grounds your actions? If the history of experience in the New World was to make the logic of freedom and absolute possession one, how do you address those you meet at the end of your vision?

Judith told me that Frears asked her without conflict—as if it were a matter of simple, empirical report—whether she would consent to be his mistress and available to him on short notice. She told me she answered yes without a second thought. Their affair lasted, she said, on and off, for three years.

Hold in your mind the results of this contemplation with the mental sound of the musical note constructed by combining the following elements from the method's three tables: *III. I. i(a); i(b)*. (Remember that the task is to devise just arguments against an imperial state that your one true love will apply to her own circumstances using this method, this juxtaposition of words and scenes.)

Extended notation from my practice: III. Historical Subject: Judith Takes (Governing scene: A young New England woman listens to a beautiful young man speaking in public about slavery on a summer evening on Nantucket in 1841. This image gives way and merges with the image of Judith approaching Charles Jason Frears in a Greenwich Village jazz club in September of 1963. She has just said, "I've brought you something for your birthday," and he, laughing gently, is saying, "You've brought me you."). I: Truth Statement: Every ruling minority needs to numb, and, if possible, to kill the time-sense of those whom it exploits by proposing a continuous present. This is the authoritarian secret of all methods of imprisonment. i(a). Constructive Principle (positive): Enlightenment ideals of individual meditative freedom are inseparable from the liberal dream of universal print literacy. i(b). Constructive Principle (negative): Historylessness was once assigned to those deemed unworthy of equality or incapable of mastering the Christian logic of redeemed American time.

Second Day's Exercise: In the Jesuits' version of this method the second day of the fourth week is devoted to imagining the two women standing in front of an open sepulcher cut into the side of a hill. The tomb's covering of un-worked stone leans at an angle as if having been rolled away by unskilled laborers. The women are listening to someone speaking: "Ye seek Jesus of Nazareth. He is not here." There is no sign of the soldiers assigned to guard the place. The dead man was tortured and killed in accordance with the provisions of the law against fomenters of disorder and disseminators of sedition. One day my brother stole something. It was not the first time. The national narrative of redemption promises the end of history as material fact in the New World. This is primitive thought. But do not think for a minute that our class does not subscribe to its premises. Our self-regard could not survive any other narrative logic but absolute possession. My pleasure of rule extends as far as yours. Nevertheless, I saw what I saw in my vision and have decided to act. In the time I have left I will live in the present the one true history of my one true love. Repeat yesterday's exercise: The juxtaposition of the governing scene for your third historical subject with the governing scene you use to call to mind easily your master narrative. Refuse empire; create reciprocity.

Hold in your mind the results of this exercise's contemplations with the imagined sound of the musical note constructed by combining the following elements from the method's three tables: *III. II. ii(a); ii(b).* Construct arguments against empire your one true love will believe.

Extended notation from my practice: III. Historical Subject: Judith Takes (Governing Scene: A nineteen-year-old woman listens to a man speaking in public about the red gate of slavery on a summer evening on Nantucket in August of 1841. This scene gives way and merges with the image of Judith approaching Charles Frears in a Greenwich Village jazz club in 1963.). II. Truth Statement: The most important element of poetics is the structure of events, for tragedy is the mimesis not of persons but of life and action. Happiness and unhappiness consist in action and the goal is a certain kind of action and not a qualitative state. It is by virtue of character that persons have certain qualities, but it is through their actions that they are happy or the reverse. ii(a). Constructive Principle (positive): It is both necessary and possible to live the one true history of your one true love. ii(b). Constructive Principle (negative): In any history of absolute possession reciprocity must be improvised moment to moment. Narrative implies direction; stories are vehicles of consent.

At the time of my vision during the music at Mary Joscelyn's funeral in 1995, I was a happily married man and father of an infant daughter. I failed to knock on Jesse Bishop's door in the spring of 1984. (I've checked and now have given the correct year.) Since 2007 I have separated from my wife and now see my daughter two nights a week and on alternate weekends. I developed this method in order to learn to live the one true history of my one true love. I declared my love to Leda Corot Rivers three weeks ago today.

I kept in touch with Judith Takes until her death last year. She always seemed much younger than her age. She died at the age of seventy.

I visited her only once toward the end. She said she wanted to say good-bye quickly. Judith wrote a much-praised book about the audiences the abolitionists addressed early in the early nineteenth century. She pointed out that this was the age of minstrelsy's greatest popularity. Each age constructs word and act and nationality much differently. She was especially interested in what the women in the audiences heard and what they made of what was said. She tried to reconstruct, as accurately as she could, who was present at the meeting on Nantucket in August of 1841, arguing that that meeting and that young man's speech signaled the potency— against all odds—of the political appeal of abolitionism.

Judith and I sometimes talked about whether American national historical subjectivity was a meaningful concept. I thought it was. She doubted it. History's events, I now think, can be given biographical temporalities or denied them. That choice, I think, is made in the imagination first.

Derek is Judith and Jason Frears's son. Judith left all her papers and her library of antislavery documents to the Frears Memorial American Music Archive. I have asked Derek to permit me to go through this material and his mother's notes to see if possibly there is enough material for a book about popular culture and antislavery that McClaren Books and NCI might agree to publish.

Colloquy delivered to the accompaniment of the third subject's second note: You were brave beyond what was expected.

I was not. I have never been in a position to sign the kind of document you wrote and signed in late December of 2004. Until I practiced this method every day for several months, I had no way to begin to know what I would do in circumstances like the ones you faced. Now I can imagine nothing stopping me. I hope something similar will happen to you.

Third Day's Exercise: Master narratives often sound as if they could tell us what to do: "Tell my disciples," Jesus told the women, "to go up to Galilee and I will appear to them there." "So they began to beat him early in the morning . . . I did not cast off the chains of slavery at the time of the surrender, they fell off at that camp meeting." Narrative should not postpone the question of justice with the promise of perfection. Make the narrative of events serve consent to being in general and not to the self-justifying techniques of domination. I'm valuable because she came back.

Place the figure of your one true love inside the governing scene you chose for your master narrative. We hold these Truths to be self-evident: All men . . . Then find a way to declare your love.

Hold in your mind the results of this exercise's contemplations with the mental sound of the musical note constructed by combining the following elements from the method's three tables: *III. III. iii(a); iii(b).*

Extended notation from my practice: III. Historical Subject: Judith Takes (Governing scene: On a summer evening on Nantucket Island in 1841, a young woman listens to a man speaking of his introduction as a child to slavery as a legal system of impunity. This moment gives way to and merges with a picture of Judith offering her love to Frears in a jazz club in Greenwich Village in 1963.). III. Truth Statement: I would like to arrive at the point where I am able to grasp the essence of a certain place and time, compose the work, and play it on the spot naturally. iii(a). Constructive Principle (positive): The most important philosophical question is the question of what Eurydice saw when Orpheus looked back. iii(b). Constructive Principle (negative): The time of the contemporary social determination of events is stochastic. This technique of managed discontinuity postpones the Enlightenment project of justice and equality continuously.

Colloquy delivered to the accompaniment of the third subject's third note: You granted torturers immunity with your signature on December 30, 2004. I have memorized what you wrote:

> Because the discussion in that memorandum concerning the President's Commander-in-Chief power and the potential defenses to liability was—and remains—unnecessary, it has been eliminated from the analysis that follows. Consideration of the bounds of any such authority would be inconsistent with the President's unequivocal directive that United States personnel not engage in torture. "Torture" means an act committed by a person acting under color of law specifically intended to inflict severe physical or mental pain or suffering (other than pain or suffering incidental to lawful sanctions) upon another person within his custody or physical control.

You were brave beyond the rule and measure of our training and learned with your body what words spoken in good faith could mean. A trainer in charge of teaching soldiers to endure being tortured by enemies stated for the record: "It's not simulated anything. Usually the person goes into hysterics on the board. Our waterboarders are professional. When the water hits you, you think, 'Oh Shit, this is a whole new level of Bad.'" Master narratives and governing scenes are not luxuries Homeland Security should be given the legal and technical means to censor and suppress to safeguard citizens' national security.

Fourth Day's Exercise: It was never customary to extend mercy to those living outside the laws of civilized nations whom we held at will, first as enemies then as property. This was always the fate to be expected by those who failed at diplomacy and arms. In my vision during the music at Mary Joscelyn's funeral service I came to the end of myself and saw other people standing there. Fathers killing sons. I immediately demanded that Owen Corliss, my closest colleague and best friend, give me the equivalent scene from his own life to the one I had just given in tears from mine.

I was valuable because she came back. I tried to make him see Melisande Chandless's face in the New Haven doorway and recognize her. Through music I was sure we could trust our memories—all of them. There were ways of hearing notes from which we could begin.

Narrate the happy ending implied by the governing scene you chose for this week's exercises. In my practice a girl listens in the New England summer evening light to a man speaking publicly of his entrance through the red gate of slavery. This scene merges with an image of Judith offering her love to Charles Jason Frears on his birthday. Frears laughs lovingly, saying, "You have brought me you." What Eurydice saw when Orpheus looked back determines the worth of his song. I failed to knock on Jesse's door in Lexington, Kentucky in the spring of 1984. When Leda sang "Light Years" in Toronto last month, I knew I could use my method and act immediately according to the knowledge gained by the promptings of desire.

Juxtapose the happy ending your governing scene implies with the happiness your master narrative intends to bring. I did not cast off the chains of slavery at the time of the surrender. They fell off at that camp meeting.

In the Jesuits' version of this method, Jesus's resurrection and public, historical ascension into heaven from Mount Olivet seal the perfection of events. It is not much knowledge that fills and satisfies the soul, but the intimate understanding and relish of the truth.

Owen Corliss refused what I asked of him. Nevertheless, I have found a way to act on the truth of vision. History and Enlightenment open onto an inner realm (operating by its own laws) without any extrinsic purposes whatsoever.

Hold in mind the results of your contemplations by constructing the mental sound of a musical note, combining the following elements from the method's three tables: *III. IV. iv(a); iv(b).* (Remember that the task is to narrate the happy ending implied by your governing scene and juxtapose it with the universal happiness your master narrative intends to complete.)

Extended notation from my practice: III. Historical Subject: Judith Takes (Governing Scene: *A young woman listens to a man speaking and imagines her own entrance through the bloodstained gate of slavery. This scene gives way and merges* with an image of Judith offering Jason Frears her love. Both Judith and Frears trust their happiness.). IV. Truth Statement: Some discouragement, some faintness of heart at the new real future that replaces the imaginary, is not unusual, and we do not expect people to be deeply moved by what is not unusual. That element of tragedy which lies in the very fact of frequency, has not yet wrought itself into the coarse emotion of mankind; and perhaps our frames could hardly bear very much of it. If we had a keen vision and feeling of all ordinary human life, it would be like hearing the grass grow and the squirrel's heart beat and we should die of that roar which lies on the other side of silence. As it is, the quickest of us walk about well wadded with stupidity. iv(a). Constructive Principle (positive): It is both necessary and possible to create a society of equal historical selves (SOEHS). iv(b). Constructive Principle (negative): All music derives its beauty from the way the notes take flight over the ground of reproach issuing from the continuous speech of all the anonymous dead.

Colloquy delivered to the accompaniment of the third subject's fourth note: If I can devise some easier, friendlier way of conveying my goodwill, I will share it with you between now and the 19th and when we are scheduled to meet.

Fifth Day's Exercise: Imagine the violence of the governing scene you have chosen with which to hold the third historical subject in mind. Then imagine the happy ending your master narrative implies for everyone. Since I have begun practicing this method, I have decided to act on desire. Leda in the midst of her singing is a braided chord, sounding aloud the actual history of my one true love.

The nature of true virtue is consent to being in general. A

history of the work of redemption in the New World implies that there will be nothing between events and words. I am valuable because she came back. This is the true nature of historical action.

Hold in your mind the results of your meditation during the exercise assigned to your third historical subject's fifth day. Do this by constructing the mental sound of the musical note made by combining the following elements from the method's three tables: *III. V. i(a); i(b).* (The task is to juxtapose the violence of the imagery you chose with the happiness the master narrative intends to achieve.)

Extended notation from my practice: III. Historical Subject: Judith Takes (Governing scene: A young woman listens to a man publicly speaking his remembrance of slavery. This scene merges with a picture of Judith declaring her love.). V. Truth Statement: Whenever events lose their independent value, an abstruse exegesis is born. i(a). Constructive Principle (positive): The emancipative dimension of bourgeois literacy implies a universality of communicative reciprocity between autonomous individuals of equal worth. History is the narrative of the fulfillment of this idea. i(b). Constructive Principle (negative): The historylessness that characterizes contemporary experience harms both individual and collective life and prevents a just reciprocity among equals.

Sixth Day's Exercise: When in December of 2004 you wrote and signed the legal memorandum permitting torture, the virtue of American historical syntax was undone. The liberal logic of slavery prevailed over nature's freedom. Music comes to us first as words that have to be discarded in the emergency of events. Narrate the happy ending your master narrative has given your third historical subject's governing scene knowing the syntax of domination is unworthy of trust. Greet your one true love as if after a long absence.

Hold in mind the results of your contemplations during this exercise with the mental sound of the musical note constructed from the following elements taken from the method's three tables: *III. VI. ii(a); ii(b).*

Extended notation from my practice: III. Historical Subject: Judith Takes (Governing scene: A woman listens while blood pours down in a child's sight to a man publicly speaking of himself as a child watching a woman suspended from a iron hook in a ceiling's wooden beam being whipped and screaming because she was loved and owned. This picture merges with an image of Judith declaring her love to a musician who has just played a love song to an audience of strangers in September of 1963.). VI. Truth Statement: When the whole world is a computer and all cultures are recorded on a single tribal drum, the fixed point of view of print culture will be irrelevant and impossible no matter how valuable. ii(a). Constructive Principle (positive): It is both necessary and possible to live the one true history of your one true love. ii(b). Constructive Principle (negative): Reciprocity must be improvised, moment-to-moment.

Colloquy delivered to the accompaniment of the fourth week's sixth note: You will soon receive (if you have not already done so) an invitation to attend, as a special guest of NCI, the public dedication on June 19th of the Charles Jason Frears Memorial American Music Archive and Performance Center just now being completed on the New Carrollton campus of the University of Maryland. I understand that your home is quite close by. I have sent you this letter and historical method in advance in the sincere hope that you will be able to attend and we will be able to find a time and place to meet.

Seventh Day's Exercise: I recently found among Judith's papers in her handwriting lyrics to Charles Jason Frears' signature composition "Light Years." I can find no evidence or anyone's anecdotal remembrance of their existence prior to my discovery. I have taken the liberty of removing this page from the collection until we are able to establish, with your firm's help, the potential commercial value that the licensing rights to these words may command.

It seems possible to me they will be ruled integral elements of the intellectual property held in "Light Years" as an original work. Owner of copyright might then be entitled to claim back royalties. I don't pretend to know the legal dimensions or ramifications of all of this. But I believe the announcement of the existence and the content of the lyrics themselves should be left to the discretion of Derek as Judith's son and heir and to the executors of the Frears estate.

In the Jesuits' version of this method the seventh day's exercise of the fourth week is reserved for contemplations of the disciple who said, "Unless I see, I will not believe." When Jesus came to him and ordered the saint to place his fingers inside the wound in his side (Jesus was tortured and killed in a manner reserved for the lowest criminals), the saint said, "My Lord and my God." Compose the lyrics of a love song to your one true love without the consolation of this happy ending.

Love Song in Imperial Time
Every moment forfeit
In this history of absolute loss:
I am valuable because she came back.

If you see Leda before I do,
Sing her this song
So she does not choose another.
I will do the same for you
If, while you are away, I meet
Your one true love
And you teach me
The words. Refuse
Empire; create reciprocity.

Hold in mind the contemplations that result from this exercise with the imagined sound of the musical note constructed by combining the following elements from the method's three tables: *IV. VII. iii(a); iii(b).*

Extended notation from my practice: III. Historical Subject: Judith Takes (Governing scene: A young woman listens to a young man speaking. This image gives way and merges with the image of Judith Takes declaring her love to a man on his birthday.). VII. Truth Statement: At first I was afraid. This familiar music demanded action of the kind of which I was incapable, and yet, had I lingered there beneath the surface I might have attempted to act. Nevertheless, I know now that few really listen to this music. iii(a). Constructive Principle (positive): A serious philosophical question of our time is the question of what Eurydice saw when Orpheus looked back. iii(b). Constructive Principle (negative): Stochastic temporality makes private, individual, and public events appear separate and incommensurate. Enlightenment reciprocity between equals, anticipated in literacy, implies a temporality past domination. Compose notes for a historical song that move beyond the constraints of what is without appeal to transcendence of any kind.

FIRST TWO DAYS OF THE FIFTH WEEK

It is to be strongly recommended that the two days remaining to complete the first cycle of this method be devoted to reviewing the method's rules and to a close scrutiny of the three documents I have appended. (In addition to the newspaper article containing the biography of George Anderson and the official text of your memorandum of December 30, 2004, I have included a transcript of my love letter to Leda, written and delivered February 5, 2010.) Remember that in subsequent cycles of this method, you will be asked to make yourself the historical subject of the fourth week's exercises.

DOCUMENTS

GEORGE ANDERSON

Interviewed, 1925, New Jersey,
by Marion C. MacRobert

Age: one hundred eight
b. 1817, Virginia
Enslaved: Virginia
Field hand

Up at 501 Calhoun street there is a little, weather-beaten frame house that sets back from the sidewalk, huddled between two large properties as though trying to hide its shabbiness from the gaze of the passerby. The busy public has no time to take a second look at it, so few know its secret. It is the home of one to Trenton's very richest men.

His wealth does not consist of anything so commonplace as money. If he wanted a dollar right this minute it is extremely doubtful if he could find it anywhere in those worn old clothes of his, but he has a store house, and in it are treasures that only a man who has lived a whole century may possess—it is the storehouse of memory.

While he pursued the humble calling of a farmer time went marching by, leaving in its wake the history of three wars and the advent of the greatest triumphs of a scientific age. Best of all, from his point of view, time brought the abolishment of slavery, treasure of treasures for the storehouse. Now that age has robbed him of his once healthy body he can fall back upon this wealth and distribute it to those about him, and, after all, no man is quite so rich as the man who shares.

He is George Anderson, colored, a former slave, whose family records show him to be 108 years old. He lives with his daughter, Mrs. Fannie Coleman, who was a little girl when the Civil War ended, and whose grandchild, Cora Edna, a plump little kiddie with feet forever keeping time to some imaginary tune, is "uncle George's" constant companion.

Uncle George is unable to walk because his poor old legs crumple up when he puts the weight of his feeble old body upon them, so that he spends the greater part of his time sitting on the side of his bed. But his eyes are bright and his memory very good. Now and then during a conversation his mind will wander off into by-paths and must be brought back sharply, but with careful handling he can tell a straightforward story of his youth and of the years before and after "the surrendah," as he speaks of the end of the Civil War.

BORN IN SLAVERY

Born in slavery on a plantation near Danville, Va., he knew no other life until he was 46, when the slaves were freed. If his lot was a hard one he did not realize it; slaves were slaves and masters were masters, and between them there was no question of freedom for the black man. He was owned as his master's mules and other stock were owned.

Slaves were meant to be beaten if they deserved it, and Uncle George witnessed beatings time and again, escaping them himself because he had worked out a plan of his own and found it good. He knew whippings hurt terribly, found it out when he was a very little boy and saw how the slaves suffered under the lash. But always there was an excuse back of the flogging, the colored man had stolen or committed some other misdemeanor, or he had shirked at his labor.

"If I do what I am told," he said to himself, "and never do the things the other folks are punished for, they'll never need to beat me." He held to this maxim and is thankful that among his recollections there is not one of the feel of the lash.

Uncle George has a wonderfully soft voice and the mellow accent of the southern reared Negro, the tone and accent that cannot be reproduced on paper. His voice grows softer still as he tells of one episode in his life that he wishes he could forget.

"My master was a minister," he told the writer, "he was a strict man who preached every Saturday and Sunday and on the other days gave his attention to the farm. If he thought a black man needed flogging he'd tie him to a post and do it himself if the overseer was busy. One day my brother stole something. It was not the first time; he had been punished for it before, and the master said that this time he should have a lesson he would never forget. So they began to beat him early in the morning, and when his back was all cut open they put salt on it and pounded it in with a paddle. Then they whipped him again, and when the overseer's arm would get tired the master would take the whip. By and by, late in the afternoon, my brother did not cry out anymore, just swayed from side to side, side to side, going lower all the time until he went down and did not come up again. 'That ought to settle him for good,' said the master. 'He'll never steal again.' My brother didn't, for they had beaten him to death."

Uncle George said he did not feel any special resentment against the master. He had known slaves to be beaten to death before and his brother was only another one, but he lived in fear of the whipping post and for this reason made himself the most docile of servants.

He married a slave woman and began to raise a family and when he was in the early forties he heard of the war being fought to give slaves their freedom. It didn't interest him much, for he was reasonably satisfied with his lot. There was enough to eat and a place to sleep, and he and his family were clothed after a fashion. In winter they suffered with cold, but the winter was short and there were long months of sunshine. There was no waste on the big plantation, he says. The slaves were fed whatever was most plentiful, and sometimes their fare consisted only of buttermilk, which they drank from great wooden tubs. Their eating implements were usually mussel shells, easy to find and to replace. They were a healthy lot, and contented, and never gave freedom a thought. Uncle George was considered too old to go along with the southern troops as a handyman, though a few of the younger slaves from the plantation were sent.

After a time came disturbing news, and then long lines of tired men in gray straggling back to their homes. Lee had "surrendahed," the cause of the south was lost. Mrs. Coleman remembers seeing the soldiers return. She was a tiny little girl and the memory is not very distinct, but it is there. Nothing had been said to Uncle George about his freedom and he didn't ask about it, but news drifted in now and then, and finally great droves of negroes passed the plantation singing as they went.

FREEDOM

"Come on," they shouted to Uncle George one day. "We's got freedom." But before he could answer them the master walked out of the door with a club in his hand.

"Don't bring any of that d——— freedom inside my gates," he yelled to them, and they didn't.

Nothing more was said to the plantation negroes, but one day several weeks later, the master went to Uncle George and told him that he was no longer a slave.

"I will give you all records about yourself," he said, "and you must put them in a safe place. You were just 46 years old at the time of the surrender. You were born on the plantation. You needn't stay here unless you want to. I need you as much as ever and if you want to stay and work, I will pay you."

So life went on much as before except that now and then the Negroes received a small sum of money. When the master died Uncle George found a little farm of his own where he worked harder than ever and where his boys and girls finished growing up. By and by, wife and children were gone and then Mrs. Coleman sent for him. He farmed for a time near New Hope and is still a member of a church there.

He declares until he came north he never knew that it was possible for colored folks to live as comfortably as whites.

"Up here," he says, "I have always had enough to eat; enough clothes to keep me warm; a dry roof over my head and peace and comfort."

Though he is unable to move about, his days are by no means unoccupied. He likes to sew, and he always takes care of his own clothes in addition to helping with the family mending. When a needle is ready to be threaded, the bright eyes of Cora Edna are at his service.

There is one subject of conversation of which he never tires. He is a devout Christian and his faith is beautiful. He can quote chapter after chapter from the Bible, and God is very real and very near to him. Let those who will discuss evolution, the divinity of Christ, virgin birth or any of the other things that tend to contradict the things in the wonderful old Book. Uncle George accepts it all literally, and in his opinion there is not room for one question. He likes to tell how he was converted at a Southern camp meeting many years ago.

"When I knew I had found my Savior I got right up in that meeting and told everybody so," he explains; "and since that time I have never been alone. I did not cast off the chains of slavery at the time of the surrender, they fell off at that camp meeting."

The aged man has another firm belief, and will listen to no arguments to the contrary. He believes that he started to die three times. His feet went first, he says, and then death crept up to his knees and on steadily toward his heart. But the staunch old heart refused to even hesitate and then death crept away again baffled.

"Sometime it will come again," says Uncle George, "and I'll go on up to Heaven."

Such is the faith of the man whom it is believed is Trenton's oldest citizen. It may be just as well to explain that the accompanying picture was taken some time ago, possibly on his 100th anniversary. Great age is now written plainly on his face and form and there seems to be no reason to doubt the correctness of the old master's record, which says that Uncle George was 46 years old "time of the surrendah." [Trenton *State Gazette*, April 6, 1925.]

December 30, 2004
MEMORANDUM OPINION FOR THE DEPUTY ATTORNEY GENERAL

Torture is abhorrent both to American law and values and to international norms. This universal repudiation of torture is reflected in our criminal law, for example, 18 U.S.C. §§ 2340-2340A; international agreements, exemplified by the United Nations Convention Against Torture (the "CAT")[1]; customary international law[2]; centuries of Anglo-American law[3]; and the longstanding policy of the United States, repeatedly and recently reaffirmed by the President.[4]

This Office interpreted the federal criminal prohibition against torture—codified at 18 U.S.C. §§ 2340-2340A—in *Standards of Conduct for Interrogation under 18 U.S.C. §§ 2340-2340A* (Aug. 1, 2002) ("August 2002 Memorandum"). The August 2002 Memorandum also addressed a number of issues beyond interpretation of those statutory provisions, including the President's Commander-in-Chief power, and various defenses that might be asserted to avoid potential liability under sections 2340-2340A. See *id.* at 31-46.

Questions have since been raised, both by this Office and by others, about the appropriateness and relevance of the non-statutory discussion in the August 2002 Memorandum, and also about various aspects of the statutory analysis, in particular the statement that "severe" pain under the statute was limited to pain "equivalent in intensity to the pain accompanying serious physical injury, such as organ failure, impairment of bodily function, or even death." *Id.* at 1.[5] We decided to withdraw the August 2002 Memorandum, a decision you announced in June 2004. At that time, you directed this Office to prepare a replacement memorandum. Because of the importance of—and public interest in—these issues, you asked that this memorandum be prepared in a form that could be released to the public so that interested parties could understand our analysis of the statute.

This memorandum supersedes the August 2002 Memorandum in its entirety.[6] Because the discussion in that memorandum concerning the President's Commander-in-Chief power and the potential defenses to liability was—and remains—unnecessary, it has been eliminated from the analysis that follows. Consideration of the bounds of any such authority would be inconsistent with the President's unequivocal directive that United States personnel not engage in torture.[7]

We have also modified in some important respects our analysis of the legal standards applicable under 18 U.S.C. §§ 2340-2340A. For example, we disagree with statements in the August 2002 Memorandum limiting "severe" pain under the statute to "excruciating and agonizing" pain, *id.* at 19, or to pain "equivalent in intensity to the pain accompanying serious physical injury, such as organ failure, impairment of bodily function, or even death," *id.* at 1. There are additional areas where we disagree with or modify the analysis in the August 2002 Memorandum, as identified in the discussion below.[8]

The Criminal Division of the Department of Justice has reviewed this memorandum and concurs in the analysis set forth below.

I.

Section 2340A provides that "[w]hoever outside the United States commits or attempts to commit torture shall be fined under this title or imprisoned not more than 20 years, or both, and if death results to any person from conduct prohibited by this subsection, shall be punished by death or imprisoned for any term of years or for life."[9] Section 2340(1) defines "torture" as "an act committed by a person acting under the color of law specifically intended to inflict severe physical or mental pain or suffering (other than pain or suffering incidental to lawful sanctions) upon another person within his custody or physical control."[10]

In interpreting these provisions, we note that Congress may have adopted a statutory definition of "torture" that differs from certain colloquial uses of the term. Cf. *Cadet v. Bulger*, 377 F.3d 1173, 1194 (11th Cir. 2004) ("[I]n other contexts and under other definitions [the conditions] might be described as torturous. The fact remains, however, that the only relevant definition of 'torture' is the definition contained in [the] CAT. . . ."). We must, of course, give effect to the statute as enacted by Congress.[11]

Congress enacted sections 2340-2340A to carry out the United States' obligations under the CAT. *See* H.R. Conf. Rep. No. 103-482, at 229 (1994). The CAT, among other things, obligates state parties to take effective measures to prevent acts of torture in any territory under their jurisdiction, and requires the United States, as a state party, to ensure that acts of torture, along with attempts and complicity to commit such acts, are crimes under U.S. law. *See* CAT arts. 2, 4-5. Sections 2340-2340A satisfy that requirement with respect to acts committed outside the United States.[12] Conduct constituting "torture" occurring within the United States was—and remains—prohibited by various other federal and state criminal statutes that we do not discuss here.

The CAT defines "torture" so as to require the intentional infliction of "severe pain or suffering, whether physical or mental." Article 1(1) of the CAT provides:

> For the purposes of this Convention, the term "torture" means any act by which severe pain or suffering, whether physical or mental, is intentionally inflicted on a person for such purposes as obtaining from him or a third person information or a confession, punishing him for an act he or a third person has committed or is suspected of having committed, or intimidating or coercing him or a third person, or for any reason based on discrimination of any kind, when such pain or suffering is inflicted by or at the instigation of or with the consent or acquiescence of a public official or other person acting in an official capacity. It does not include pain or suffering arising only from, inherent in or incidental to lawful sanctions.

The Senate attached the following understanding to its resolution of advice and consent to ratification of the CAT:

> The United States understands that, in order to constitute torture, an act must be specifically intended to inflict severe physical or mental pain or suffering and that mental pain or suffering

refers to prolonged mental harm caused by or resulting from (1) the intentional infliction or threatened infliction of severe physical pain or suffering; (2) the administration or application, or threatened administration or application, of mind altering substances or other procedures calculated to disrupt profoundly the senses or the personality; (3) the threat of imminent death; or (4) the threat that another person will imminently be subjected to death, severe physical pain or suffering, or the administration or application of mind altering substances or other procedures calculated to disrupt profoundly the senses or personality.

S. Exec. Rep. No. 101-30, at 36 (1990). This understanding was deposited with the U.S. instrument of ratification, see 1830 U.N.T.S. 320 (Oct. 21, 1994), and thus defines the scope of the United States' obligations under the treaty. *See Relevance of Senate Ratification History to Treaty Interpretation*, 11 Op. O.L.C. 28, 32-33 (1987). The criminal prohibition against torture that Congress codified in 18 U.S.C. §§ 2340-2340A generally tracks the prohibition in the CAT, subject to the U.S. understanding.

II.

Under the language adopted by Congress in sections 2340-2340A, to constitute "torture," the conduct in question must have been "specifically intended to inflict severe physical or mental pain or suffering." In the discussion that follows, we will separately consider each of the principal components of this key phrase: (1) the meaning of "severe"; (2) the meaning of "severe physical pain or suffering"; (3) the meaning of "severe mental pain or suffering"; and (4) the meaning of "specifically intended."

(1) The meaning of "severe."

Because the statute does not define "severe," "we construe [the] term in accordance with its ordinary or natural meaning." *FDIC v. Meyer*, 510 U.S. 471, 476 (1994). The common understanding of the term "torture" and the context in which the statute was enacted also inform our analysis.

Dictionaries define "severe" (often conjoined with "pain") to mean "extremely violent or intense: *severe pain." American Heritage Dictionary of the English Language* 1653 (3d ed. 1992); *see also XV Oxford English Dictionary 101* (2d ed. 1989) ("Of pain, suffering, loss, or the like: Grievous, extreme" and "Of circumstances . . . : Hard to sustain or endure").[13]

The statute, moreover, was intended to implement the United States' obligations under the CAT, which, as quoted above, defines as "torture" acts that inflict "severe pain or suffering" on a person. CAT art. 1(1). As the Senate Foreign Relations Committee explained in its report recommending that the Senate consent to ratification of the CAT:

The [CAT] seeks to define "torture" in a relatively limited fashion, corresponding to the common understanding of torture as an extreme practice which is universally condemned. . . .

. . . .

. . . The term "torture," in United States and international usage, is usually reserved for extreme, deliberate and unusually cruel practices, for example, sustained systematic beating, application of electric currents to sensitive parts of the body, and tying up or hanging in positions that cause extreme pain.

S. Exec. Rep. No. 101-30, at 13-14. *See also* David P. Stewart, *The Torture Convention and the Reception of International Criminal Law Within the United States*, 15 Nova L. Rev. 449, 455 (1991) ("By stressing the extreme nature of torture, . . . [the] definition [of torture in the CAT] describes a relatively limited set of circumstances likely to be illegal under most, if not all, domestic legal systems.").

Further, the CAT distinguishes between torture and "other acts of cruel, inhuman or degrading treatment or punishment which do not amount to torture as defined in article 1." CAT art. 16. The CAT thus treats torture as an "extreme form" of cruel, inhuman, or degrading treatment. See S. Exec. Rep. No. 101-30, at 6, 13; *see also* J. Herman Burgers & Hans Danelius, *The United Nations Convention Against Torture: A Handbook on the Convention Against Torture and Other Cruel, Inhuman or Degrading Treatment or Punishment* 80 (1988) ("*CAT Handbook*") (noting that Article 16 implies "that torture is the *gravest form* of [cruel, inhuman, or degrading] treatment [or] punishment") (emphasis added); Malcolm D. Evans, *Getting to Grips with Torture*, 51 Int'l & Comp. L.Q. 365, 369 (2002) (The CAT "formalises a distinction between torture on the one hand and inhuman and degrading treatment on the other by attributing different legal consequences to them.").[14] The Senate Foreign Relations Committee emphasized this point in its report recommending that the Senate consent to ratification of the CAT. *See S. Exec. Rep.* No. 101-30, at 13 ("'Torture' is thus to be distinguished from lesser forms of cruel, inhuman, or degrading treatment or punishment, which are to be deplored and prevented, but are not so universally and categorically condemned as to warrant the severe legal consequences that the Convention provides in the case of torture. . . . The requirement that torture be an extreme form of cruel and inhuman treatment is expressed in Article 16, which refers to 'other acts of cruel, inhuman or degrading treatment or punishment *which do not amount to torture* . . . .'"). *See also Cadet*, 377 F.3d at 1194 ("The definition in CAT draws a critical distinction between 'torture' and 'other acts of cruel, inhuman, or degrading punishment or treatment.'").

Representations made to the Senate by Executive Branch officials when the Senate was considering the CAT are also relevant in interpreting the CAT's torture prohibition—which sections 2340-2340A implement. Mark Richard, a Deputy Assistant Attorney General in the Criminal Division, testified that "[t]orture is understood to be that barbaric cruelty which lies at the top of the pyramid of human rights misconduct." *Convention Against Torture: Hearing Before the Senate Comm. on Foreign Relations*, 101st Cong. 16 (1990) ("*CAT Hearing*") (prepared statement). The Senate Foreign

Relations Committee also understood torture to be limited in just this way. *See S. Exec. Rep. No.* 101-30, at 6 (noting that "[f]or an act to be 'torture,' it must be an extreme form of cruel and inhuman treatment, causing severe pain and suffering, and be intended to cause severe pain and suffering"). Both the Executive Branch and the Senate acknowledged the efforts of the United States during the negotiating process to strengthen the effectiveness of the treaty and to gain wide adherence thereto by focusing the Convention "on torture rather than on other relatively less abhorrent practices." *Letter of Submittal from George P. Shultz, Secretary of State, to President Ronald Reagan* (May 10, 1988), in S. Treaty Doc. No. 100-20, at v; *see also* S. Exec. Rep. No. 101-30, at 2-3 ("The United States" helped to focus the Convention "on torture rather than other less abhorrent practices."). Such statements are probative of a treaty's meaning. *See* 11 Op. O.L.C. at 35-36.

Although Congress defined "torture" under sections 2340-2340A to require conduct specifically intended to cause "severe" pain or suffering, we do not believe Congress intended to reach only conduct involving "excruciating and agonizing" pain or suffering. Although there is some support for this formulation in the ratification history of the CAT,[15] a proposed express understanding to that effect[16] was "criticized for setting too high a threshold of pain," S. Exec. Rep. No. 101-30, at 9, and was not adopted. We are not aware of any evidence suggesting that the standard was raised in the statute and we do not believe that it was.[17]

Drawing distinctions among gradations of pain (for example, severe, mild, moderate, substantial, extreme, intense, excruciating, or agonizing) is obviously not an easy task, especially given the lack of any precise, objective scientific criteria for measuring pain.[18] We are, however, aided in this task by judicial interpretations of the Torture Victims Protection Act ("TVPA"), 28 U.S.C. § 1350 note (2000). The TVPA, also enacted to implement the CAT, provides a civil remedy to victims of torture. The TVPA defines "torture" to include:

> any act, directed against an individual in the offender's custody or physical control, by which *severe pain or suffering* (other than pain or suffering arising only from or inherent in, or incidental to, lawful sanctions), *whether physical or mental,* is intentionally inflicted on that individual for such purposes as obtaining from that individual or a third person information or a confession, punishing that individual for an act that individual or a third person has committed or is suspected of having committed, intimidating or coercing that individual or a third person, or for any reason based on discrimination of any kind . . . .

28 U.S.C. § 1350 note, § 3(b)(1) (emphases added). The emphasized language is similar to section 2340's "severe physical or mental pain or suffering."[19] As the Court of Appeals for the District of Columbia Circuit has explained:

> The severity requirement is crucial to ensuring that the conduct proscribed by the [CAT] and the TVPA is sufficiently extreme and outrageous to warrant the universal condemnation that the term "torture" both connotes and invokes. The

drafters of the [CAT], as well as the Reagan Administration that signed it, the Bush Administration that submitted it to Congress, and the Senate that ultimately ratified it, therefore all sought to ensure that "only acts of a certain gravity shall be considered to constitute torture."

The critical issue is the degree of pain and suffering that the alleged torturer intended to, and actually did, inflict upon the victim. The more intense, lasting, or heinous the agony, the more likely it is to be torture.

Price v. Socialist People's Libyan Arab Jamahiriya, 294 F.3d 82, 92-93 (D.C. Cir. 2002) (citations omitted). That court concluded that a complaint that alleged beatings at the hands of police but that did not provide details concerning "the severity of plaintiffs' alleged beatings, including their frequency, duration, the parts of the body at which they were aimed, and the weapons used to carry them out," did not suffice "to ensure that [it] satisf[ied] the TVPA's rigorous definition of torture." *Id.* at 93.

In *Simpson v. Socialist People's Libyan Arab Jamahiriya*, 326 F.3d 230 (D.C. Cir. 2003), the D.C. Circuit again considered the types of acts that constitute torture under the TVPA definition. The plaintiff alleged, among other things, that Libyan authorities had held her incommunicado and threatened to kill her if she tried to leave. *See id.* at 232, 234. The court acknowledged that "these alleged acts certainly reflect a bent toward cruelty on the part of their perpetrators," but, reversing the district court, went on to hold that "they are not in themselves so unusually cruel or sufficiently extreme and outrageous as to constitute torture within the meaning of the [TVPA]." *Id.* at 234. Cases in which courts have found torture suggest the nature of the extreme conduct that falls within the statutory definition. *See, e.g., Hilao v. Estate of Marcos*, 103 F.3d 789, 790-91, 795 (9th Cir. 1996) (concluding that a course of conduct that included, among other things, severe beatings of plaintiff, repeated threats of death and electric shock, sleep deprivation, extended shackling to a cot (at times with a towel over his nose and mouth and water poured down his nostrils), seven months of confinement in a "suffocatingly hot" and cramped cell, and eight years of solitary or near-solitary confinement, constituted torture); *Mehinovic v. Vuckovic*, 198 F. Supp. 2d 1322, 1332-40, 1345-46 (N.D. Ga. 2002) (concluding that a course of conduct that included, among other things, severe beatings to the genitals, head, and other parts of the body with metal pipes, brass knuckles, batons, a baseball bat, and various other items; removal of teeth with pliers; kicking in the face and ribs; breaking of bones and ribs and dislocation of fingers; cutting a figure into the victim's forehead; hanging the victim and beating him; extreme limitations of food and water; and subjection to games of "Russian roulette," constituted torture); *Daliberti v. Republic of Iraq*, 146 F. Supp. 2d 19, 22-23 (D.D.C. 2001) (entering default judgment against Iraq where plaintiffs alleged, among other things, threats of "physical torture, such as cutting off . . . fingers, pulling out . . . fingernails," and electric shocks to the testicles); *Cicippio v. Islamic Republic of Iran*, 18 F. Supp. 2d 62, 64-66 (D.D.C. 1998) (concluding that a course of conduct that included frequent beatings, pistol whipping, threats of imminent death, electric shocks, and attempts to force confessions by playing Russian roulette and pulling the trigger at each denial, constituted torture).

(2) The meaning of "severe physical pain or suffering."

The statute provides a specific definition of "severe mental pain or suffering," *see* 18 U.S.C. § 2340(2), but does not define the term "severe physical pain or suffering." Although we think the meaning of "severe physical pain" is relatively straightforward, the question remains whether Congress intended to prohibit a category of "severe physical suffering" distinct from "severe physical pain." We conclude that under some circumstances "severe physical suffering" may constitute torture even if it does not involve "severe physical pain." Accordingly, to the extent that the August 2002 Memorandum suggested that "severe physical suffering" under the statute could in no circumstances be distinct from "severe physical pain," *id.* at 6 n.3, we do not agree.

We begin with the statutory language. The inclusion of the words "or suffering" in the phrase "severe physical pain or suffering" suggests that the statutory category of physical torture is not limited to "severe physical pain." This is especially so in light of the general principle against interpreting a statute in such a manner as to render words surplusage. *See, e.g., Duncan v. Walker*, 533 U.S. 167, 174 (2001).

Exactly what is included in the concept of "severe physical suffering," however, is difficult to ascertain. We interpret the phrase in a statutory context where Congress expressly distinguished "physical pain or suffering" from "mental pain or suffering." Consequently, a separate category of "physical suffering" must include something other than any type of "mental pain or suffering."[20] Moreover, given that Congress precisely defined "mental pain or suffering" in the statute, it is unlikely to have intended to undermine that careful definition by including a broad range of mental sensations in a "physical suffering" component of "physical pain or suffering."[21] Consequently, "physical suffering" must be limited to adverse "physical" rather than adverse "mental" sensations.

The text of the statute and the CAT, and their history, provide little concrete guidance as to what Congress intended separately to include as "severe physical suffering." Indeed, the record consistently refers to "severe physical pain or suffering" (or, more often in the ratification record, "severe physical pain *and* suffering"), apparently without ever disaggregating the concepts of "severe physical pain" and "severe physical suffering" or discussing them as separate categories with separate content. Although there is virtually no legislative history for the statute, throughout the ratification of the CAT—which also uses the disjunctive "pain or suffering" and which the statutory prohibition implements—the references were generally to "pain *and* suffering," with no indication of any difference in meaning. *The Summary and Analysis of the Convention Against Torture and Other Cruel, Inhuman or Degrading Treatment or Punishment*, which appears in S. Treaty Doc. No. 100-20, at 3, for example, repeatedly refers to "pain *and* suffering." *See also* S. Exec. Rep. No. 101-30, at 6 (three uses of "pain and suffering"); *id.* at 13 (eight uses of "pain and suffering"); *id.* at 14 (two uses of "pain and suffering"); *id.* at 35 (one use of "pain and suffering"). Conversely, the phrase "pain or suffering" is used less frequently in the Senate report in discussing (as opposed to quoting) the CAT and the understandings under consideration, *e.g., id.* at 5-6 (one use of "pain or suffering"), *id.* at 14 (two uses of "pain or suffering"); *id.* at 16 (two uses of "pain or suffering"), and, when used, it is with no suggestion that it has any different meaning.

Although we conclude that inclusion of the words "or suffering" in "severe physical pain or suffering" establishes that physical torture is not limited to "severe physical pain," we also conclude that Congress did not intend "severe physical pain or suffering" to include a category of "physical suffering" that would be so broad as to negate the limitations on the other categories of torture in the statute. Moreover, the "physical suffering" covered by the statute must be "severe" to be within the statutory prohibition. We conclude that under some circumstances "physical suffering" may be of sufficient intensity and duration to meet the statutory definition of torture even if it does not involve "severe physical pain." To constitute such torture, "*severe* physical suffering" would have to be a condition of some extended duration or persistence as well as intensity. The need to define a category of "severe physical suffering" that is different from "severe physical pain," and that also does not undermine the limited definition Congress provided for torture, along with the requirement that any such physical suffering be "severe," calls for an interpretation under which "severe physical suffering" is reserved for physical distress that is "severe" considering its intensity and duration or persistence, rather than merely mild or transitory.[22] Otherwise, the inclusion of such a category would lead to the kind of uncertainty in interpreting the statute that Congress sought to reduce both through its understanding to the CAT and in sections 2340-2340A.

(3) The meaning of "severe mental pain or suffering."

Section 2340 defines "severe mental pain or suffering" to mean:

the prolonged mental harm caused by or resulting from—

(A) the intentional infliction or threatened infliction of severe physical pain or suffering;

(B) the administration or application, or threatened administration or application, of mind-altering substances or other procedures calculated to disrupt profoundly the senses or the personality;

(C) the threat of imminent death; or

(D) the threat that another person will imminently be subjected to death, severe physical pain or suffering, or the administration or application of mind-altering substances or other procedures calculated to disrupt profoundly the senses or personality[.]

18 U.S.C. § 2340(2). Torture is defined under the statute to include an act specifically intended to inflict severe mental pain or suffering. *Id.* § 2340(1).

An important preliminary question with respect to this definition is whether the statutory list of the four "predicate acts" in section 2340(2)(A)-(D) is exclusive. We conclude that Congress intended the list of predicate acts to be exclusive—that is, to constitute the proscribed "severe mental pain or suffering" under the statute, the prolonged mental harm must be caused by acts falling within one of the four statutory categories of predicate acts. We reach this conclusion based on the clear language of the statute, which provides a detailed definition that includes four categories of predicate acts joined by the disjunctive and does not contain a catchall provision or any other language suggesting that additional acts might qualify (for example, language such as "including" or "such acts as").[23] Congress plainly considered very specific predicate acts, and this definition tracks the Senate's understanding concerning mental pain or suffering when giving its advice and consent to ratification of the CAT. The conclusion that the list of predicate acts is exclusive is consistent with both the text of the Senate's understanding, and with the fact that it was adopted out of concern that the CAT's definition of torture did not otherwise meet the requirement for clarity in defining crimes. *See supra* note 21. Adopting an interpretation of the statute that expands the list of predicate acts for "severe mental pain or suffering" would constitute an impermissible rewriting of the statute and would introduce the very imprecision that prompted the Senate to adopt its understanding when giving its advice and consent to ratification of the CAT.

Another question is whether the requirement of "prolonged mental harm" caused by or resulting from one of the enumerated predicate acts is a separate requirement, or whether such "prolonged mental harm" is to be presumed any time one of the predicate acts occurs. Although it is possible to read the statute's reference to "*the* prolonged mental harm caused by or resulting from" the predicate acts as creating a statutory presumption that each of the predicate acts always causes prolonged mental harm, we do not believe that was Congress's intent. As noted, this language closely tracks the understanding that the Senate adopted when it gave its advice and consent to ratification of the CAT:

> in order to constitute torture, an act must be specifically intended to inflict severe physical or mental pain or suffering and that mental pain or suffering refers to prolonged mental harm caused by or resulting from (1) the intentional infliction or threatened infliction of severe physical pain or suffering; (2) the administration or application, or threatened administration or application, of mind altering substances or other procedures calculated to disrupt profoundly the senses or the personality; (3) the threat of imminent death; or (4) the threat that another person will imminently be subjected to death, severe physical pain or suffering, or the administration or application of mind altering substances or other procedures calculated to disrupt profoundly the senses or personality.

S. Exec. Rep. No. 101-30, at 36. We do not believe that simply by adding the word "the" before "prolonged harm," Congress intended a material change in the definition of mental pain or suffering as articulated in the Senate's understanding to the CAT. The legislative history, moreover, confirms that sections 2340-2340A were intended to fulfill—but not go beyond—the United States' obligations under the CAT: "This section provides the necessary legislation to implement the [CAT]. . . . The definition of torture emanates directly from article 1 of the [CAT]. The definition for 'severe mental pain and suffering' incorporates the [above mentioned] understanding." S. Rep. No. 103-107, at 58-59 (1993). This understanding, embodied in the statute, was meant to define the obligation undertaken by the United States. Given this understanding, the legislative history, and the fact that section 2340(2) defines "severe mental pain or suffering" carefully in language very similar to the understanding, we do not believe that Congress intended the definition to create a presumption that any time one of the predicate acts occurs, prolonged mental harm is deemed to result.

Turning to the question of what constitutes "prolonged mental harm caused by or resulting from" a predicate act, we believe that Congress intended this phrase to require mental "harm" that is caused by or that results from a predicate act, and that has some lasting duration. There is little guidance to draw upon in interpreting this phrase.[24] Nevertheless, our interpretation is consistent with the ordinary meaning of the statutory terms. First, the use of the word "harm"—as opposed to simply repeating "pain or suffering"—suggests some mental damage or injury. Ordinary dictionary definitions of "harm," such as "physical or mental *damage: injury,*" *Webster's Third New International Dictionary* at 1034 (emphasis added), or "[p]hysical or psychological *injury or damage,*" *American Heritage Dictionary of the English Language* at 825 (emphasis added), support this interpretation. Second, to "prolong" means to "lengthen in time" or to "extend in duration," or to "draw out," *Webster's Third New International Dictionary* at 1815, further suggesting that to be "prolonged," the mental damage must extend for some period of time. This damage need not be permanent, but it must continue for a "prolonged" period of time.[25] Finally, under section 2340(2), the "prolonged mental harm" must be "caused by" or "resulting from" one of the enumerated predicate acts.[26]

Although there are few judicial opinions discussing the question of "prolonged mental harm," those cases that have addressed the issue are consistent with our view. For example, in the TVPA case of *Mehinovic*, the court explained that:

> [The defendant] also caused or participated in the plaintiffs' mental torture. Mental torture consists of "prolonged mental harm caused by or resulting from: the intentional infliction or threatened infliction of severe physical pain or suffering; . . . the threat of imminent death . . . ." As set out above, plaintiffs noted in their testimony that they feared that they would be killed by [the defendant] during the beatings he inflicted or during games of "Russian roulette." *Each plaintiff continues to suffer long-term psychological harm as a result of the ordeals they suffered at the hands of defendant and others.*

198 F. Supp. 2d at 1346 (emphasis added; first ellipsis in original). In reaching its conclusion, the court noted that the plaintiffs were continuing to suffer serious mental harm even ten years after the events in question: One plaintiff "suffers from anxiety, flashbacks, and nightmares and has difficulty sleeping. [He] continues to suffer thinking about what happened to him during this ordeal and has been unable to work as a result of the continuing effects of the torture he endured." *Id.* at 1334. Another plaintiff "suffers from anxiety, sleeps very little, and has frequent nightmares. . . . [He] has found it impossible to return to work." *Id.* at 1336. A third plaintiff "has frequent nightmares. He has had to use medication to help him sleep. His experience has made him feel depressed and reclusive, and he has not been able to work

since he escaped from this ordeal." *Id.* at 1337-38. And the fourth plaintiff "has flashbacks and nightmares, suffers from nervousness, angers easily, and has difficulty trusting people. These effects directly impact and interfere with his ability to work." *Id.* at 1340. In each case, these mental effects were continuing years after the infliction of the predicate acts.

And in *Sackie v. Ashcroft,* 270 F. Supp. 2d 596 (E.D. Pa. 2003), the individual had been kidnapped and "forcibly recruited" as a child soldier at the age of 14, and over the next three to four years had been forced to take narcotics and threatened with imminent death. *Id.* at 597-98, 601-02. The court concluded that the resulting mental harm, which continued over this three-to-four-year period, qualified as "prolonged mental harm." *Id.* at 602.

Conversely, in *Villeda Aldana v. Fresh Del Monte Produce, Inc.*, 305 F. Supp. 2d 1285 (S.D. Fla. 2003), the court rejected a claim under the TVPA brought by individuals who had been held at gunpoint overnight and repeatedly threatened with death. While recognizing that the plaintiffs had experienced an "ordeal," the court concluded that they had failed to show that their experience caused lasting damage, noting that "there is simply no allegation that Plaintiffs have suffered any prolonged mental harm or physical injury as a result of their alleged intimidation." *Id.* at 1294-95.

(4) The meaning of "specifically intended."

It is well recognized that the term "specific intent" is ambiguous and that the courts do not use it consistently. *See* 1 Wayne R. LaFave, *Substantive Criminal Law* § 5.2(e), at 355 & n.79 (2d ed. 2003). "Specific intent" is most commonly understood, however, "to designate a special mental element which is required above and beyond any mental state required with respect to the *actus reus* of the crime." *Id.* at 354; *see also Carter v. United States*, 530 U.S. 255, 268 (2000) (explaining that general intent, as opposed to specific intent, requires "that the defendant possessed knowledge [only] with respect to the *actus reus* of the crime"). As one respected treatise explains:

> With crimes which require that the defendant intentionally cause a specific result, what is meant by an "intention" to cause that result? Although the theorists have not always been in agreement . . . , the traditional view is that a person who acts . . . intends a result of his act . . . under two quite different circumstances: (1) when he consciously desires that result, whatever the likelihood of that result happening from his conduct; and (2) when he knows that that result is practically certain to follow from his conduct, whatever his desire may be as to that result.

1 LaFave, *Substantive Criminal Law*, § 5.2(a), at 341 (footnote omitted).

As noted, the cases are inconsistent. Some suggest that only a conscious desire to produce the proscribed result constitutes specific intent; others suggest that even reasonable foreseeability suffices. In *United States v. Bailey*, 444 U.S. 394 (1980), for example, the Court suggested that, at least "[i]n a general sense," *id.* at 405, "specific intent" requires that one consciously desire the result. *Id.* at 403-05. The Court compared the common law's *mens rea* concepts of specific intent and general intent to the Model Penal Code's *mens rea* concepts of acting purposefully and acting knowingly. *Id.* at 404-05. "[A] person who causes a particular result is said to act purposefully," wrote the Court, "if 'he consciously desires that result, whatever the likelihood of that result happening from his conduct.'" *Id.* at 404 (internal quotation marks omitted). A person "is said to act knowingly," in contrast, "if he is aware 'that that result is practically certain to follow from his conduct, whatever his desire may be as to that result.'" *Id.* (internal quotation marks omitted). The Court then stated: "In a general sense, 'purpose' corresponds loosely with the common-law concept of specific intent, while 'knowledge' corresponds loosely with the concept of general intent." *Id.* at 405.

In contrast, cases such as *United States v. Neiswender*, 590 F.2d 1269 (4th Cir. 1979), suggest that to prove specific intent it is enough that the defendant simply have "knowledge or notice" that his act "would have likely resulted in" the proscribed outcome. *Id.* at 1273. "Notice," the court held, "is provided by the reasonable foreseeability of the natural and probable consequences of one's acts." *Id.*

We do not believe it is useful to try to define the precise meaning of "specific intent" in section 2340.[27] In light of the President's directive that the United States not engage in torture, it would not be appropriate to rely on parsing the specific intent element of the statute to approve as lawful conduct that might otherwise amount to torture. Some observations, however, are appropriate. It is clear that the specific intent element of section 2340 would be met if a defendant performed an act and "consciously desire[d]" that act to inflict severe physical or mental pain or suffering. 1 LaFave, *Substantive Criminal Law* § 5.2(a), at 341. Conversely, if an individual acted in good faith, and only after reasonable investigation establishing that his conduct would not inflict severe physical or mental pain or suffering, it appears unlikely that he would have the specific intent necessary to violate sections 2340-2340A. Such an individual could be said neither consciously to desire the proscribed result, *see, e.g., Bailey,* 444 U.S. at 405, nor to have "knowledge or notice" that his act "would likely have resulted in" the proscribed outcome, *Neiswender,* 590 F.2d at 1273.

Two final points on the issue of specific intent: First, specific intent must be distinguished from motive. There is no exception under the statute permitting torture to be used for a "good reason." Thus, a defendant's motive (to protect national security, for example) is not relevant to the question whether he has acted with the requisite specific intent under the statute. *See Cheek v. United States,* 498 U.S. 192, 200-01 (1991). Second, specific intent to take a given action can be found even if the defendant will take the action only conditionally. *Cf., e.g., Holloway v. United States,* 526 U.S. 1, 11 (1999) ("[A] defendant may not negate a proscribed intent by requiring the victim to comply with a condition the defendant has no right to impose."). *See also id.* at 10-11 & nn. 9-12; Model Penal Code § 2.02(6). Thus, for example, the fact that a victim might have avoided being tortured by cooperating with the perpetrator would not make permissible actions otherwise constituting torture under the statute. Presumably that has frequently been the case with torture, but that fact does not make the practice of torture any less abhorrent or unlawful.[28]

——

1. Convention Against Torture and Other Cruel, Inhuman or Degrading Treatment or Punishment, Dec. 10, 1984, S. Treaty Doc. No. 100-20, 1465 U.N.T.S. 85. *See also, e.g.,* International Covenant on Civil and Political Rights, Dec. 16, 1966, 999 U.N.T.S. 171.

2. It has been suggested that the prohibition against torture has achieved the status of *jus cogens* (i.e., a peremptory norm) under international law. *See, e.g., Siderman de Blake v. Republic of Argentina,* 965 F.2d 699, 714 (9th Cir. 1992); *Regina v. Bow Street Metro. Stipendiary Magistrate Ex Parte Pinochet Ugarte (No. 3),* [2000] 1 AC 147, 198; *see also* Restatement (Third) of Foreign Relations Law of the United States § 702 reporters' note 5.

3. *See generally* John H. Langbein, *Torture and the Law of Proof: Europe and England in the Ancien Régime* (1977).

4. *See, e.g.,* Statement on United Nations International Day in Support of Victims of Torture, 40 Weekly Comp. Pres. Doc. 1167 (July 5, 2004) ("Freedom from torture is an inalienable human right . . . ."); Statement on United Nations International Day in Support of Victims of Torture, 39 Weekly Comp. Pres. Doc. 824 (June 30, 2003) ("Torture anywhere is an affront to human dignity everywhere."); *see also Letter of Transmittal from President Ronald Reagan to the Senate* (May 20, 1988), *in Message from the President of the United States Transmitting the Convention Against*

Torture and Other Cruel, Inhuman or Degrading Treatment or Punishment, S. Treaty Doc. No. 100-20, at iii (1988) ("Ratification of the Convention by the United States will clearly express United States opposition to torture, an abhorrent practice unfortunately still prevalent in the world today.").

5. *See, e.g.*, Anthony Lewis, *Making Torture Legal*, N.Y. Rev. of Books, July 15, 2004; R. Jeffrey Smith, *Slim Legal Grounds for Torture Memos*, Wash. Post, July 4, 2004, at A12; Kathleen Clark & Julie Mertus, *Torturing the Law; the Justice Department's Legal Contortions on Interrogation*, Wash. Post, June 20, 2004, at B3; Derek Jinks & David Sloss, *Is the President Bound by the Geneva Conventions?*, 90 Cornell L. Rev. 97 (2004).

6. This memorandum necessarily discusses the prohibition against torture in sections 2340-2340A in somewhat abstract and general terms. In applying this criminal prohibition to particular circumstances, great care must be taken to avoid approving as lawful any conduct that might constitute torture. In addition, this memorandum does not address the many other sources of law that may apply, depending on the circumstances, to the detention or interrogation of detainees (for example, the Geneva Conventions; the Uniform Code of Military Justice, 10 U.S.C. § 801 et seq.; the Military Extraterritorial Jurisdiction Act, 18 U.S.C. §§ 3261-3267; and the War Crimes Act, 18 U.S.C. § 2441, among others). Any analysis of particular facts must, of course, ensure that the United States complies with all applicable legal obligations.

7. *See, e.g.*, Statement on United Nations International Day in Support of Victims of Torture, 40 Weekly Comp. Pres. Doc. 1167-68 (July 5, 2004) ("America stands against and will not tolerate torture. We will investigate and prosecute all acts of torture . . . in all territory under our jurisdiction. . . . Torture is wrong no matter where it occurs, and the United States will continue to lead the fight to eliminate it everywhere.").

8. While we have identified various disagreements with the August 2002 Memorandum, we have reviewed this Office's prior opinions addressing issues involving treatment of detainees and do not believe that any of their conclusions would be different under the standards set forth in this memorandum.

9. Section 2340A provides in full:

> (a) Offense.—Whoever outside the United States commits or attempts to commit torture shall be fined under this title or imprisoned not more than 20 years, or both, and if death results to any person from conduct prohibited by this subsection, shall be punished by death or imprisoned for any term of years or for life.
>
> (b) Jurisdiction.—There is jurisdiction over the activity prohibited in subsection (a) if—
>
> > (1) the alleged offender is a national of the United States; or
> >
> > (2) the alleged offender is present in the United States, irrespective of the nationality of the victim or alleged offender.
>
> (c) Conspiracy.—A person who conspires to commit an offense under this section shall be subject to the same penalties (other than the penalty of death) as the penalties prescribed for the offense, the commission of which was the object of the conspiracy.

18 U.S.C. § 2340A (2000).

10. Section 2340 provides in full:

As used in this chapter—

(1) "torture" means an act committed by a person acting under color of law specifically intended to inflict severe physical or mental pain or suffering (other than pain or suffering incidental to lawful sanctions) upon another person within his custody or physical control;

(2) "severe mental pain or suffering" means the prolonged mental harm caused by or resulting from—

(A) the intentional infliction or threatened infliction of severe physical pain or suffering;

(B) the administration or application, or threatened administration or application, of mind-altering substances or other procedures calculated to disrupt profoundly the senses or the personality;

(C) the threat of imminent death; or

(D) the threat that another person will imminently be subjected to death, severe physical pain or suffering, or the administration or application of mind-altering substances or other procedures calculated to disrupt profoundly the senses or personality; and

(3) "United States" means the several States of the United States, the District of Columbia, and the commonwealths, territories, and possessions of the United States.

18 U.S.C. § 2340 (as amended by Pub. L. No. 108-375, 118 Stat. 1811 (2004)).

11. Our task is only to offer guidance on the meaning of the statute, not to comment on policy. It is of course open to policymakers to determine that conduct that might not be prohibited by the statute is nevertheless contrary to the interests or policy of the United States.

12. Congress limited the territorial reach of the federal torture statute, providing that the prohibition applies only to conduct occurring "outside the United States," 18 U.S.C. § 2340A(a), which is currently defined in the statute to mean outside "the several States of the United States, the District of Columbia, and the commonwealths, territories, and possessions of the United States." Id. § 2340(3).

13. Common dictionary definitions of "torture" further support the statutory concept that the pain or suffering must be severe. *See Black's Law Dictionary* 1528 (8th ed. 2004) (defining "torture" as "[t]he infliction of *intense pain* to the body or mind to punish, to extract a confession or information, or to obtain sadistic pleasure") (emphasis added); *Webster's Third New International Dictionary of the English Language Unabridged* 2414 (2002) (defining "torture" as "the infliction of *intense pain* (as from burning, crushing, wounding) to punish or coerce someone") (emphasis added); *Oxford American Dictionary and Language Guide* 1064 (1999) (defining "torture" as "the infliction of *severe bodily pain,* esp. as a punishment or a means of persuasion") (emphasis added).

This interpretation is also consistent with the history of torture. *See generally* the descriptions in Lord Hope's lecture, *Torture,* University of Essex/Clifford Chance Lecture 7-8 (Jan. 28, 2004), and in Professor Langbein's book, *Torture and the Law of Proof: Europe and England in the Ancien Régime.* We emphatically are not saying that only such historical techniques—or similar ones—can constitute "torture" under sections

2340-2340A. But the historical understanding of "torture" is relevant to interpreting Congress's intent. *Cf. Morissette v. United States*, 342 U.S. 246, 263 (1952).

14. This approach—distinguishing torture from lesser forms of cruel, inhuman, or degrading treatment—is consistent with other international law sources. The CAT's predecessor, the U.N. Torture Declaration, defined torture as "an *aggravated* and deliberate form of cruel, inhuman or degrading treatment or punishment." Declaration on the Protection of All Persons from Being Subjected to Torture and Other Cruel, Inhuman or Degrading Treatment or Punishment, U.N. Res. 3452, art. 1(2) (Dec. 9, 1975) (emphasis added); *see also* S. Treaty Doc. No. 100-20 at 2 (The U.N. Torture Declaration was "a point of departure for the drafting of the [CAT]."). Other treaties also distinguish torture from lesser forms of cruel, inhuman, or degrading treatment. *See, e.g.*, European Convention for the Protection of Human Rights and Fundamental Freedoms, art. 3, 213 U.N.T.S. 221 (Nov. 4, 1950) ("European Convention") ("No one shall be subjected to torture or to inhuman or degrading treatment or punishment."); Evans, *Getting to Grips with Torture*, 51 Int'l & Comp. L.Q. at 370 ("[T]he ECHR organs have adopted . . . a 'vertical' approach . . . , which is seen as comprising three separate elements, each representing a progression of seriousness, in which one moves progressively from forms of ill-treatment which are 'degrading' to those which are 'inhuman' and then to 'torture'. The distinctions between them is [sic] based on the severity of suffering involved, with 'torture' at the apex."); Debra Long, Association for the Prevention of Torture, *Guide to Jurisprudence on Torture and Ill-Treatment: Article 3 of the European Convention for the Protection of Human Rights* 13 (2002) (The approach of distinguishing between "torture," "inhuman" acts, and "degrading" acts has "remained the standard approach taken by the European judicial bodies. Within this approach torture has been singled out as carrying a special stigma, which distinguishes it from other forms of ill-treatment."). *See also CAT Handbook* at 115-17 (discussing the European Court of Human Rights

("ECHR") decision in *Ireland v. United Kingdom*, 25 Eur. Ct. H.R. (ser. A) (1978) (concluding that the combined use of wall-standing, hooding, subjection to noise, deprivation of sleep, and deprivation of food and drink constituted inhuman or degrading treatment but not torture under the European Convention)). Cases decided by the ECHR subsequent to *Ireland* have continued to view torture as an aggravated form of inhuman treatment. *See, e.g., Aktas v. Turkey*, No. 24351/94 ¶ 313 (E.C.H.R. 2003); *Akkoc v. Turkey*, Nos. 22947/93 & 22948/93 ¶ 115 (E.C.H.R. 2000); *Kaya v. Turkey*, No. 22535/93 ¶ 117 (E.C.H.R. 2000).

The International Criminal Tribunal for the Former Yugoslavia ("ICTY") likewise considers "torture" as a category of conduct more severe than "inhuman treatment." *See, e.g., Prosecutor v. Delalic*, IT-96-21, Trial Chamber Judgment ¶ 542 (ICTY Nov. 16, 1998) ("[I]nhuman treatment is treatment which deliberately causes serious mental and physical suffering that falls short of the severe mental and physical suffering required for the offence of torture.").

15. Deputy Assistant Attorney General Mark Richard testified: "[T]he essence of torture" is treatment that inflicts "excruciating and agonizing physical pain." *CAT Hearing* at 16 (prepared statement).

16. *See* S. Treaty Doc. No. 100-20, at 4-5 ("The United States understands that, in order to constitute torture, an act must be a deliberate and calculated act of an extremely cruel and inhuman nature, specifically intended to inflict excruciating and agonizing physical or mental pain or suffering.").

17. Thus, we do not agree with the statement in the August 2002 Memorandum that "[t]he Reagan administration's understanding that the pain be 'excruciating and agonizing' is in substance not different from the Bush administration's proposal that the pain must be severe." August 2002 Memorandum at 19. Although the terms are concededly imprecise,

and whatever the intent of the Reagan Administration's understanding, we believe that in common usage "excruciating and agonizing" pain is understood to be more intense than "severe" pain.

The August 2002 Memorandum also looked to the use of "severe pain" in certain other statutes, and concluded that to satisfy the definition in section 2340, pain "must be equivalent in intensity to the pain accompanying serious physical injury, such as organ failure, impairment of bodily function, or even death." *Id.* at 1; *see also id.* at 5-6, 13, 46. We do not agree with those statements. Those other statutes define an "emergency medical condition," for purposes of providing health benefits, as "a condition manifesting itself by acute symptoms of sufficient severity (including severe pain)" such that one could reasonably expect that the absence of immediate medical care might result in death, organ failure or impairment of bodily function. *See, e.g.*, 8 U.S.C. § 1369 (2000); 42 U.S.C. § 1395w-22(d)(3)(B) (2000); *id.* § 1395dd(e) (2000). They do not define "severe pain" even in that very different context (rather, they use it as an indication of an "emergency medical condition"), and they do not state that death, organ failure, or impairment of bodily function cause "severe pain," but rather that "severe pain" may indicate a condition that, if untreated, could cause one of those results. We do not believe that they provide a proper guide for interpreting "severe pain" in the very different context of the prohibition against torture in sections 2340-2340A. *Cf. United States v. Cleveland Indians Baseball Co.*, 532 U.S. 200, 213 (2001) (phrase "wages paid" has different meaning in different parts of Title 26); *Robinson v. Shell Oil Co.*, 519 U.S. 337, 343-44 (1997) (term "employee" has different meanings in different parts of Title VII).

18. Despite extensive efforts to develop objective criteria for measuring pain, there is no clear, objective, consistent measurement. As one publication explains:

Pain is a complex, subjective, perceptual phenomenon with a number of dimensions—intensity, quality, time course, impact, and personal meaning—that are uniquely experienced by each individual and, thus, can only be assessed indirectly. *Pain is a subjective experience and there is no way to objectively quantify it.* Consequently, assessment of a patient's pain depends on the patient's overt communications, both verbal and behavioral. Given pain's complexity, one must assess not only its somatic (sensory) component but also patients' moods, attitudes, coping efforts, resources, responses of family members, and the impact of pain on their lives.

Dennis C. Turk, *Assess the Person, Not Just the Pain*, Pain: Clinical Updates, Sept. 1993 (emphasis added). This lack of clarity further complicates the effort to define "severe" pain or suffering.

19. Section 3(b)(2) of the TVPA defines "mental pain or suffering" similarly to the way that section 2340(2) defines "severe mental pain or suffering."

20. Common dictionary definitions of "physical" confirm that "physical suffering" does not include mental sensations. *See, e.g., American Heritage Dictionary of the English Language* at 1366 ("Of or relating to the body as distinguished from the mind or spirit"); *Oxford American Dictionary and Language Guide* at 748 ("of or concerning the body (*physical exercise; physical education*)").

21. This is particularly so given that, as Administration witnesses explained, the limiting understanding defining mental pain or suffering was considered necessary to avoid problems of vagueness. *See, e.g.*, CAT Hearing at 8, 10 (prepared statement of Abraham Sofaer, Legal Adviser, Department of State: "The Convention's wording . . . is not in all respects as precise as we believe necessary. . . . [B]ecause [the Convention] requires establishment of

criminal penalties under our domestic law, we must pay particular attention to the meaning and interpretation of its provisions, especially concerning the standards by which the Convention will be applied as a matter of U.S. law. . . . [W]e prepared a codified proposal which . . . clarifies the definition of mental pain and suffering."); *id.* at 15-16 (prepared statement of Mark Richard: "The basic problem with the Torture Convention—one that permeates all our concerns—is its imprecise definition of torture, especially as that term is applied to actions which result solely in mental anguish. This definitional vagueness makes it very doubtful that the United States can, consistent with Constitutional due process constraints, fulfill its obligation under the Convention to adequately engraft the definition of torture into the domestic criminal law of the United States."); *id.* at 17 (prepared statement of Mark Richard: "Accordingly, the Torture Convention's vague definition concerning the mental suffering aspect of torture cannot be resolved by reference to established principles of international law. In an effort to overcome this unacceptable element of vagueness in Article I of the Convention, we have proposed an understanding which defines severe mental pain constituting torture with sufficient specificity to . . . meet Constitutional due process requirements.").

22. Support for concluding that there is an extended temporal element, or at least an element of persistence, in "severe physical suffering" as a category distinct from "severe physical pain" may also be found in the prevalence of concepts of "endurance" of suffering and of suffering as a "state" or "condition" in standard dictionary definitions. *See, e.g., Webster's Third New International Dictionary* at 2284 (defining "suffering" as "the endurance of or submission to affliction, pain, loss"; "a pain endured"); *Random House Dictionary of the English Language* 1901 (2d ed. 1987) ("the state of a person or thing that suffers"); *Funk & Wagnalls New Standard Dictionary of the English Language* 2416 (1946) ("A state of anguish or pain"); *American Heritage Dictionary of the English Language* at 1795 ("The condition of one who suffers").

23. These four categories of predicate acts "are members of an 'associated group or series,' justifying the inference that items not mentioned were excluded by deliberate choice, not inadvertence." *Barnhart v. Peabody Coal Co.*, 537 U.S. 149, 168 (2003) (quoting *United States v. Vonn*, 535 U.S. 55, 65 (2002)). *See also, e.g., Leatherman v. Tarrant County Narcotics Intelligence & Coordination Unit*, 507 U.S. 163, 168 (1993); 2A Norman J. Singer, *Statutes and Statutory Construction* § 47.23 (6th ed. 2000). Nor do we see any "contrary indications" that would rebut this inference. *Vonn*, 535 U.S. at 65.

24. The phrase "prolonged mental harm" does not appear in the relevant medical literature or elsewhere in the United States Code. The August 2002 Memorandum concluded that to constitute "prolonged mental harm," there must be "significant psychological harm of significant duration, e.g., lasting for months or even years." *Id.* at 1; *see also id.* at 7. Although we believe that the mental harm must be of some lasting duration to be "prolonged," to the extent that that formulation was intended to suggest that the mental harm would have to last for at least "months or even years," we do not agree.

25. For example, although we do not suggest that the statute is limited to such cases, development of a mental disorder—such as post-traumatic stress disorder or perhaps chronic depression—could constitute "prolonged mental harm." *See* American Psychiatric Association, *Diagnostic and Statistical Manual of Mental Disorders* 369-76, 463-68 (4th ed. 2000) ("DSM-IV-TR"). *See also, e.g., Report of the Special Rapporteur on Torture and Other Cruel, Inhuman or Degrading Treatment or Punishment*, U.N. Doc. A/59/324, at 14 (2004) ("The most common diagnosis of psychiatric symptoms among torture survivors is said to be post-traumatic stress disorder."); *see also* Metin Basoglu et al., *Torture and Mental Health: A Research Overview, in* Ellen Gerrity et al. eds., *The Mental Health Consequences of Torture* 48-49 (2001) (referring to findings of higher rates of post-traumatic stress disorder in studies involving torture survivors); Murat Parker et al., *Psychological Effects of Torture: An Empirical Study of Tortured and Non-Tortured Non-Political*

Prisoners, in Metin Basoglu ed., *Torture and Its Consequences: Current Treatment Approaches* 77 (1992) (referring to findings of post-traumatic stress disorder in torture survivors).

26. This is not meant to suggest that, if the predicate act or acts continue for an extended period, "prolonged mental harm" cannot occur until after they are completed. Early occurrences of the predicate act could cause mental harm that could continue—and become prolonged—during the extended period the predicate acts continued to occur. For example, in *Sackie v. Ashcroft,* 270 F. Supp. 2d 596, 601-02 (E.D. Pa. 2003), the predicate acts continued over a three-to-four-year period, and the court concluded that "prolonged mental harm" had occurred during that time.

27. In the August 2002 Memorandum, this Office concluded that the specific intent element of the statute required that infliction of severe pain or suffering be the defendant's "precise objective" and that it was not enough that the defendant act with knowledge that such pain "was reasonably likely to result from his actions" (or even that that result "is certain to occur"). *Id.* at 3-4. We do not reiterate that test here.

28. In the August 2002 Memorandum, this Office indicated that an element of the offense of torture was that the act in question actually result in the infliction of severe physical or mental pain or suffering. *See id.* at 3. That conclusion rested on a comparison of the statute with the CAT, which has a different definition of "torture" that requires the actual infliction of pain or suffering, and we do not believe that the statute requires that the defendant actually inflict (as opposed to act with the specific intent to inflict) severe physical or mental pain or suffering. *Compare* CAT art. 1(1) ("the term 'torture' means any act by which severe pain or suffering, whether physical or mental, *is intentionally inflicted*") (emphasis added) *with* 18 U.S.C. § 2340 ("'torture' means an act . . . *specifically intended to inflict* severe physical or mental pain or suffering") (emphasis added). It is unlikely that any such requirement would make any practical difference, however, since the statute also criminalizes attempts to commit torture. *Id.* § 2340A(a).

Letter

February 5, 2010

Dear Leda,

I have found no counter-narrative that is not complicit in the history we are living of absolute possession and perfect loss.

Still, in your singing there is time itself and the grace of unformed reciprocity. No event has been completed.

History creates an unformed future out of love's immediacy: I'm valuable because she came back. Make reading this into love's requited listening.

All my love to you and yours,
Theo Fales

Author's Note

More than thirty years ago I did research in early nineteenth-century records looking for evidence that recorded ordinary Americans' understanding of the history they were living. Like most historians, I found I could not use most of what I found and read. There were a surprising number of preserved attempts by townspeople of New England, both men and women, to trace in writing for their posterity the grand, mysterious, Providential arc of the history they had been living that so recently had ended in Revolution and nationhood. But most of these documents, not surprisingly perhaps, broke off abruptly, ending almost before they could begin. There was a disturbing incoherence about them I was unable to summarize or subject to interpretation. Most proclaimed soaring, happy ambitions but then shut down almost immediately after their optimistic openings. This, at least, is how I now remember them.

My research was part of an effort to recover an American sense of history before the dominance exercised by the triumphant narrative of a redeeming national American greatness became popularly established with the success of George Bancroft's multi-volume *History of the United States, from the Discovery of the American Continent* that began to be published in 1834. I have been convinced for a long time now that Americans lack a language adequate to the history we are living. This lack, I believe, is catastrophic and due in some large measure to the subjective internalization of that historical narrative of national triumph.

I have tried to write a novel that explores this condition of what I believe is a national narrative failure. The success of my ambition, it seems to me, will rest upon the reader's response to my invention of a form that purports to create the internal imaginative condition for the refusal of American national triumph—and a determination to live, love, and speak without compromise from the ground of that refusal, no matter how estranged or estranging the results may seem at first.

Having lived now for some time with the sounds and speech such an invented form made possible within me, I am reminded of those early nineteenth-century documents. Once, I despaired at my inability to interpret those earlier attempts at historical form, but when I think back on them now, I feel strangely comforted.

The seven "truth statements," so crucial to the practice of Theo Fales's historical method, are taken from the following authors and works:

I.   John Berger, *G.*
II.   Aristotle, *Poetics*
III. John Coltrane (from an interview conducted in 1965)
IV.   George Eliot, *Middlemarch*
V.   Erich Auerbach, *Dante: Poet of the Secular World*
VI.   Marshall McLuhan (from a letter to a friend written in 1959)
VII. Ralph Ellison, *Invisible Man*

In addition to the passages used verbatim from the historical documents that are printed at the end of Theo's method, the passage describing a child's witness of the torture whipping of an African American woman is taken verbatim from Frederick Douglass's *Narrative of the Life of Frederick Douglass, an American Slave.*

Peter Dimock has long worked in publishing—at Random House, and as senior executive editor for history and political science at Columbia University Press, where he worked with authors including Angela Davis, Eric Hobsbawm, Toni Morrison, and Amartya Sen. His first novel, *A Short Rhetoric for Leaving the Family*, was published by Dalkey Archive Press in 1998.

SELECTED DALKEY ARCHIVE TITLES

FOR A FULL LIST OF PUBLICATIONS, VISIT:
www.dalkeyarchive.com

SELECTED DALKEY ARCHIVE TITLES